The Lightbulb Forest

ALI HOUSE

Published in Canada by Engen Books, St. John's, NL.

Library and Archives Canada Cataloguing in Publication

Title: The lightbulb forest / Ali House.
Other titles: Short stories. Selections
Names: House, Ali, 1982- author.
Description: Short stories.
Identifiers: Canadiana (print) 20190237813 | Canadiana (ebook) 2019023797X | ISBN 9781989473313
   (softcover) | ISBN 9781989473320 (PDF)
Classification: LCC PS8615.O867 A6 2020 | DDC C813/.6—dc23

Distributed by:
Engen Books
www.engenbooks.com
submissions@engenbooks.com

First mass market paperback printing: February 2020

Cover Image: Kit Sora Photography
Interal Images: Ellen Curtis

The Lightbulb Forest

THE COLLECTED SHORT FICTION OF ALI HOUSE

ENGEN BOOKS

TABLE OF CONTENTS

THRILLER

DRAMATIC FICTION

SCIENCE FICTION

The Lightbulb Forest

It lies deep within the woods, further than you think, but closer than it seems. There is no map, nor one particular way to find it. Gaining entrance is easier than you'd believe. Secret passwords, solving riddles, humming musical notes, pretending that you don't want to find it – all have succeed at one time or another.

The change can be subtle, but eventually you'll notice that your surroundings are slowly starting to change. The once unremarkable trees are different. The colour of the bark is a strange shade of brown and seems almost leathery. The shape of the leaves is wrong, they look too square and awkward. The light streaming through the branches is reflecting off unseen objects hidden within the leaves.

Take a closer look and you'll see that the leaves are shaped like pages from a book, with lined veins and words written in a strange cursive that only nature knows how to read. Hidden among them are strange flowers, round and translucent, about the size of your palm. They look like they would break if you dared to touch them.

You can feel the cool air, hear the whisper of wind through the leaves, and see the faint shimmer of the strange flowers. There are more trees here than anticipated stretching out in all directions, further than your eyes can see.

Then you notice it. Half-hidden amongst the leaves,

one of the flowers has begun to shine, glowing brighter with each second. As you walk closer, you see that the bulb has lit up like the sun, and you are filled with a warmth unlike anything else. You could stand there and bask in the light forever, but you know that the light will not last forever. Reaching out, you find the branch this flower is on and free it from the tree. It separates easily and you hold it gently in your hands.

Some people don't make it out of the forest without incident. Sometimes their flower starts to dim and they have to be even more careful and thoughtful, so that it doesn't lose its light entirely. Sometimes it goes completely dark and all that stands before them is an inky blackness with no escape in sight. Sometimes they aren't careful and the flower breaks before they make it home, shattering into a million pieces that no longer fit together.

But if you are careful and lucky, the light will shine as long as you need, and the warmth will fill your heart and mind.

And maybe one day you will find yourself in the forest and before you will be hundreds of flowers brilliantly lit up, beckoning you to stay.

FANTASY

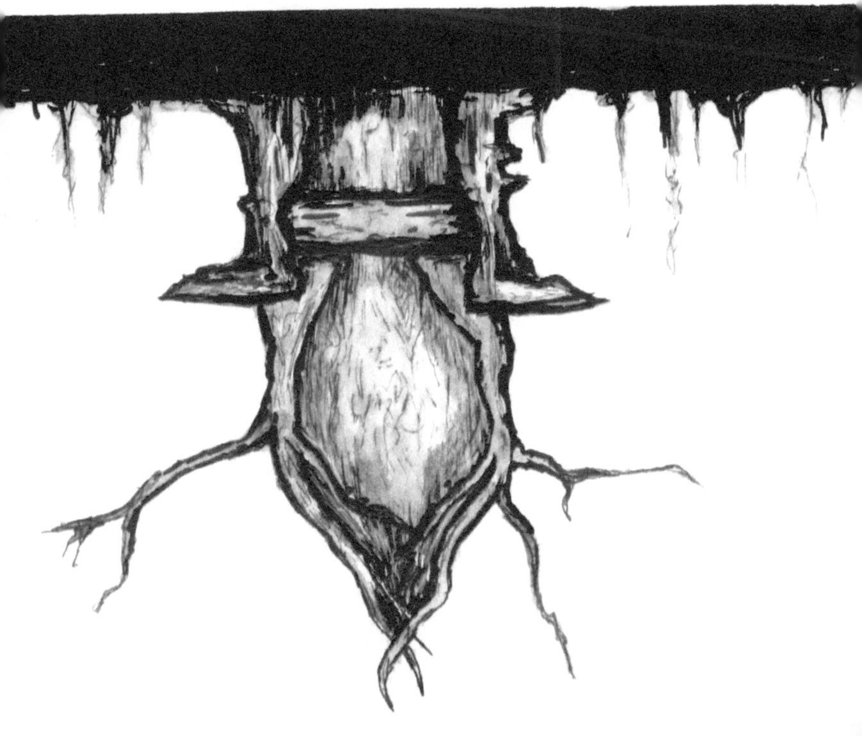

The Risk of Dreaming

As I looked out over the cliff's edge, at the vast ocean waters below, my thoughts turned to Icarus. I'd learned about him at a young age, thanks to a book of Greek myths that my aunt had gifted me on my eighth birthday. The story said that Icarus and his father had been unfairly imprisoned on the island of Crete by King Minos, and in order to escape, his father made them wondrous wings of feathers and wax. Before taking off, his father warned him that if they flew too low, the water would make the feathers too heavy to fly, and if they flew too high, the sun would melt the wax that held everything together. Icarus listened intently, but as they flew away, he became so enamoured of being up in the sky, that he didn't heed his father's warnings and flew higher and higher, getting so close to the sun that he melted the wax and fell into the sea. It was a children's book, so it didn't touch on Icarus' mortality, but I learned the whole story a few years later.

It probably wasn't the best subject to be thinking about at this particular moment, but the sun was shining, the sky was clear, and I was preparing to fly.

The design was my own invention, inspired in parts by a bicycle, a kite, and birds. I'd spent over a year working on it, starting with smaller models and testing them rigorously before working my way up to a full-sized prototype. Once I'd built it there was still a lot of trial and error, but I never lost hope. Every test offered new knowledge, more confidence, and brought me closer to my dream.

Months were spent testing my craft over and over, racing down hills and jumping off small ledges, gliding on the wind like a bird. After each successful trip, I'd search for a higher ledge, but eventually I ran out of places to jump from. I considered my parent's roof, but it would have been impossible to get the craft up there. Besides, the angle was all wrong.

Finally, I realized what I had to do. I had to take a risk.

Standing at the cliff's edge, I steeled my nerves. It was a long way down, but the weather was ideal, the wind was strong, and my craft had been tested. There was no better time than now.

"You've got this!" Eliza cheered enthusiastically. "It's gonna be great!"

Jimmy opened his mouth to say something, but then thought better and closed it.

Jimmy wasn't a fan of my ambition, but he was an only child and had inherited his mother's constant worrying. He'd fretted about this plan every step of the way, worried about what would happen if I fell or if the craft broke apart. Despite this, I could see in his eyes that there was a part of him that wanted to fly just as much as I did.

Meanwhile, Eliza was as excited as I was, if not more. She supported all of my crazy ideas, and if my craft had an extra seat, she'd be right next to me. Eliza was the fourth out of seven children, and she was the most reckless and headstrong person I knew. If it hadn't been for me, Eliza and Jimmy never would have said two words to each other, let alone been friends, but somehow I managed to bridge that gap.

They'd been present for all of my previous tests, and their input was invaluable towards making my craft better and safer. I couldn't think of anyone else I'd want with me on a day like today.

Giving the cliff's edge one last look, I walked past them and headed up the hill to where my craft sat, waiting. It looked like something out of a science fiction book, with its laid-back seat, pedals, wheels, ropes, and huge wings on top, but I had faith that it would do what I needed it to. After all, I had built many strange inventions over the years that had succeeded, despite their appearance. Lowering myself into the seat, I stretched my legs out before me and slipped them into the pedals. I did a few quick tests, making sure the chain was well connected to the wheels and that the rigging was moving the wings properly, before looking down at my friends and giving them two thumbs up.

Eliza let out a whooping sound while Jimmy gently put a hand on her arm and safely pulled her back from my intended flight path.

Putting on my helmet and lowering the goggles over my eyes, I took in a deep breath. I could see the path before me, laid out as clear as the cloudless sky above. In my imagination I had already done this hundreds of times. I would start pedalling, racing down the hill at a great enough speed that the momentum would keep me from falling into the ocean after I went over the edge. Once airborne, I'd ride the wind on those large, sturdy wings, steadying my craft, before using the ropes to tilt the wings, letting the wind lift me higher and higher. With enough skill, I'd soon be soaring far above the ground.

There were a lot of people in town who thought I was crazy. They said that I would never succeed and I should leave flying to the birds. Often they would laugh and say 'Remember Icarus!' I know that they were trying to mock me, but it was actually good advice.

See, when other people thought about the story, they focused on Icarus' fall. They considered the myth to be a warning from the gods; a reason to be satisfied with what they had, and to keep their feet firmly on the ground. If you dared to fly, then you would surely fall.

But what I thought about was Daedalus – Icarus' father. When it came to him, people only thought about what he'd lost. Yes, he'd invented something amazing, but it had cost him his only son. Still, they didn't know what his life must have been like as a prisoner, knowing that he'd never be free again. And, honestly, you can't put Icarus' death on anyone but Icarus. His father *had* warned him.

So, yes, Icarus fell, but Daedalus made it to safety. He flew over the sea and made it all the way to Sicily, finding safety from Minos. No other human had done such a thing before, but he did, wearing giant wings of feathers and wax. Daedalus lived because he understood the risk.

I thought of all my tests and theories, and everything that could go wrong.

And after that, I thought of everything that could go right.

Some people would never fly because they were too scared of falling. They would never feel the wind in their hair or gaze at the world so far down below or know that they were doing something incredible. The only way to do that was to swallow your fear and doubts, and jump. And that was exactly what I was going to do.

I took another deep breath, focused on the horizon, and prepared to fly.

Honour

Eoghan had no desire for solitude, but even he had to admit that the scene inside the tavern was a bit much. Over the past three days, he had noticed that the towns-folk here were hearty drinkers, but this was a new level of mirth. Bodies were packed into the room, barely leaving space for the tavern-keep to deliver the ale that they so desperately craved. Whenever a drink was finished, the reveller would let out a shout for more before slamming the empty vessel against the thick wooden tables – which were so used to such treatment that they could no longer dent.

Despite their many cheers, Eoghan could not make out what they were celebrating. Perhaps a battle had been won or a friend had successfully returned from a journey, or maybe they cheered simply because it was Thornsday. All around him, men and women laughed and gulped down pint after pint of mead, knocking their mugs together in triumph.

Eoghan had no desire to join the celebration, but he adhered to the customs. Whenever one of the revellers raised a glass to him and cheered, he had the good sense to follow suit. His courtesy had resulted in many smiles and a free pint from one overly mirthful man.

However, there was one who was not as accommodating to the customs. This stranger sat in the corner of the room, head bowed, completely covered by a dark, woollen cloak. Long, dark hair, clumsily cut, hung down from the hood, nearly touching the top of the table. The stranger's hands, which were wrapped around a mug, were covered by a pair of black gloves. Eoghan had been dining when the stranger came into the tavern and, despite having watched them for the past hour, could figure out nothing more about them. He could not remember seeing them look up, take a drink, or even move.

He wondered if this was the person he was looking for. For two weeks, he had been searching for a Red-Hand, but the search was not easy. One could not simply announce that they were looking for a Red-Hand without drawing suspicion. Stumbling upon such a person was not something that happened often, so Eoghan had travelled to a town where it was rumoured a Red-Hand frequented. For three days, he had been watching and waiting, and now it seemed as though his time might be at hand.

Yet he hesitated to go over to the person. What if it was not a Red-Hand and his hopes were raised and dashed for nothing? Even if it was a Red-Hand, there was no point trying to have a conversation in this environment, and Eoghan had no idea when – or if – the revels would stop. His message was not one to be had in such company. Perhaps he should find a room for the night, go to sleep, and seek out the stranger in the morning.

He had almost talked himself into leaving when it happened. A man, short and broad, raised his mug and cheered to multiple people throughout the bar. All of them cheered back, except for one. While others had been content to ignore the stranger, this man was well past reasonable thinking. Frustrated at being denied mirth, he marched over to the stranger and slammed his mug down on the table, spilling mead onto the wooden surface.

"Custom tis to cheer with others," he growled, his words slow with drink.

The stranger did not move.

"Legend say mead taste sweeter when mirth shared." He paused for a reply, but no reply was given, angering him further. "Legend also say he who refuse will come to quick end."

Such tales existed, but most people ignored them. If someone did not want to partake in celebration, then they were free to leave, and if they stayed most revellers ignored them. Nothing spoiled mirth faster than a fight to the death. This man, however, had drunk enough not to know any better.

"You cheers now?" he asked, in a low voice.

The stranger remained still and silent.

"If no cheers, then you fight and die." He removed a short hunting knife from his belt and pointed it at the stranger. The knife wavered in the air, despite the drunken man's best attempts to keep it still.

The noise died down as everyone in the tavern watched the scene unfold. Eoghan had a suspicion that the drunken man could be defeated by a simple push, but the knife looked sharp. A wild slash with that knife might cause an unexpected fatality. Then again, if the stranger was who Eoghan thought it might be, the drunken man could be in for a shock.

The drunken man stuck out his chin in an effort to look fiercer. "Look up. Need see eyes. Need see face when fighting."

The hands around the mug slowly let go. Everyone watched as the stranger carefully removed the glove and held up their right hand. The hand was slender and calloused, and the skin was dyed bright red. The room went silent.

The man put his knife away and picked up his drink. "Next time should warn," he muttered as he walked back to his friends. He gave a loud cheer and the mirth took up again – not as boisterous as before the incident, but still enough to be obnoxious.

The crowd was more than happy to ignore the stranger, but Eoghan could not tear his eyes away. Only he saw the stranger put the glove back on. Only he saw the stranger look up, revealing a long face with a scar running diagonally from forehead to cheek. The stranger frowned, her eyes quickly scanning the room before looking down again. Abandoning her drink, she stood up and exited the tavern.

All thoughts of sleep went out of Eoghan's head. Leaving his own drink behind, he quickly followed her. Night had fallen, but the moon was almost full, and it was easy enough for him to make out her cloaked form as she walked away from the tavern. It would have been easy for him to close the distance between them, but he hesitated still. He had practised his request many times, but now that he was faced with an actual Red-Hand, he was having trouble finding the words.

The stranger walked to a different tavern, one which catered to highspeak folk, and entered. Eoghan hesitated at the door. Highspeak folk always made him nervous. He considered turning away and trying to find her tomorrow, but what if she left town early and he missed this opportunity? How long would it be before another Red-Hand came to town?

No. He would do this right. He would go in this tavern, walk up to her, and state his request. The worst thing she could do was say no, although he doubted that she would turn away from such an opportunity. Taking a deep breath to steady his nerves, Eoghan pushed open the door and walked inside.

The stranger was nowhere in sight. Eoghan looked around the room many times, before finally enquiring to the tavern-keep about her. After cringing slightly at Eoghan's lowspeak, the tavern-keep confirmed that she had rented a room for the night. Eoghan rented a room for himself and paid the tavern-keep extra to let him know when the stranger awoke. The tavern-keep gave a small smile at his strange request, and he had a feeling that this was not the first time she had accepted money for such work.

Despite the comfortable mattress, it was a fitful night's sleep for Eoghan. What if the Red-Hand had noticed him following her and had ducked into the tavern to elude him? Every sound he heard made him wonder if she was slipping away under the cover of night. Eventually he fell asleep, further troubled by memories thinly disguised as dreams.

He was startled awake by a knocking on his door.

"This is your wake-up call," the tavern-keep's voice called out.

Eoghan walked over to the door and thanked her, slipping her another coin.

"Will you be breaking your fast?" the tavern-keep asked.

Eoghan considered the option. He was much too nervous to eat, but before he could reply, the tavern-keep spoke up.

"It would be a good idea to break your fast this morn."

He finally recognized the intent, and ordered some food. When he walked downstairs he noticed the Red-Hand, still fully cloaked, sitting over a plate of bread and meat. Eoghan sat a few tables away and picked at his tea and bread, stealing the occasional glance. He knew that it would be best to go over and talk to her right away, but he had not yet found the words. Besides, it was rude to interrupt someone's meal.

The Red-Hand finished eating, settled her bill, and left. As soon as she was through the door, Eoghan sprang to his feet. He tossed a few coins next to his picked-apart breakfast and hurriedly left the tavern.

She walked at a casual pace, so Eoghan was able to keep up easily. He did his best to remain hidden behind buildings and stalls as she wandered through the town, moving from stall to stall. He wondered if she was looking for anything specific, and if so, what could it be? What sort of trinkets would a Red-Hand have need to purchase?

After wandering the stalls for some time, she walked away from the town centre. It soon became apparent to Eoghan that the stranger was headed for the road out of town. He felt uneasy, for there would be no cover to hide behind. He knew that he needed to speak up, but still his words failed him, so he continued to follow.

They were barely out of the town when a stern voice called out:

"Why are you following me?"

He was confused. The stranger must have spoken, but she was still walking and had done nothing to acknowledge him. He looked around, but they were the only two people on the road. Maybe he had imagined the words?

"Speak your mind," the voice said. "Otherwise go back to where you came from and leave me be."

It had to be the stranger speaking.

Eoghan cleared his throat. "Needing your help."

"Doubtful."

He hurried his step until he was beside her. "Know what you are. Needing your help."

She stopped walking. "If you know what I am, then you should know to leave me alone. We don't like being bothered."

He took a deep breath and steadied his nerves. "Know you are Red-Hand. Know you kill for pay. Know you are best for helping."

She sighed. "If you must lowspeak, at least give me some details of what I am supposed to help you with."

"Need... Needing a murder," he said, his voice shaking.

"Obviously."

"Easy job," he added.

"And what if I do not want to be hired?"

"Pays well."

"Murder always does."

Eoghan wrung his hands. He was doing a terrible job explaining himself. Never had he imagined that a Red-Hand would be versed in highspeak.

"Easy job. Person not fight. Promise."

She looked at him and raised an eyebrow. "How would this person not fight back? Are they an Eversleep?"

He shook his head. "Is me."

She was silent. Her shoulders relaxed as she crossed her arms and took another look at him.

Eoghan cleared his throat again. "Client is me. Want you to murder me."

"Well, that is... unorthodox." She smiled. "Okay, you have made me curious. Tell me your story."

"Story? Not murder?"

"If you want me to kill you, then first you must tell me your story."

He looked around at the trees and dirt road. "Here? Now?"

She shook her head. "We will go back into town. I think the both of us could use a drink."

On her last word, she turned back to town and started walking. Not once did she look back to make sure that he was following.

They went to the highspeak tavern that they had left just a few hours earlier. The Red-Hand settled them at a table in the corner, away from the others. The gesture was appreciated by Eoghan. He was nervous about telling his story, but at least he could be certain that nobody would overhear them.

As they waited for their drinks, the Red-Hand sat quietly. Eoghan distracted himself by looking around the great room. It was much like the other tavern, only better. The smell of cooked meat and bread filled the room, mingling with the scent of exotic spices. There were two fires to sit beside, and the wooden tables and chairs were covered in ornamental carvings. He doubted that revellers would be allowed through the door.

The tavern-keep placed two mugs on their table, smiled, and walked away.

"Speak now," the Red-Hand said, picking up her mug. "I know you are a lowspeaker, but do try to make it comprehensible."

Eoghan nodded. "Am low-born, but family not poor. Had builder status – crude but dependable. Was learning trade, but not skilled like sister and brother. Was first-born, but trade did not come natural. Had to work much harder." He paused to take a drink. "Had first job by self. Made door for tavern. Door failed and tavern-keep killed by thief. Dishonoured family name. No longer have family name." He hung his head. "Want honour back, but too scared. Need you do it for me."

She was quiet for a while. He hoped that she had been able to follow his story.

"So..." she began, "you think that killing yourself is the best option?"

He nodded. "Is best. Is only way to regain lost honour."

"Really?"

He was confused. Was there another way he did not know of?

She took a long drink. "Did you ever think that maybe you were not cut out for building?"

"Is family trade, so is only trade."

"So there is nothing else that you could possibly do?

He shook his head. "Must follow family trade."

She leaned forward. "Do you think that my family's trade was murder?"

He did not respond. He knew nothing of her past. Maybe it was.

"My father's trade was translation. A rare gift – one that I learned because I was surrounded by it. My father had other trades, however, that I refused to learn or tolerate, no matter how strong the blood between us was – trades that hurt people and caused harm." She paused to finish the last of her mead. "And that is why I killed him."

Eoghan felt a chill run down his spine. He had heard that Red-Hands bragged about their kills or bemoaned them, but this was more like stating a fact.

"So are you sure you want to die?" she asked. "What if you could find a trade better suited to your skills?"

Eoghan shook his head for what felt like the hundredth time. "No skill. Only honour. Will pay well."

She frowned. "If killing yourself for honour is so important, why do you need to hire me? Why not do it yourself?"

"Tried to..." He swallowed hard and looked down at the table, remembering the night he had held a knife to his throat and tried to will his hand to draw it across. "Not strong enough. Need someone else."

When he looked up, she was studying him silently. After a minute, she raised a hand and gestured for another drink. Eoghan wondered if she was considering his option or if she was merely playing with him. He had no idea if she would say yes. She should – it was an easy job and paid well – but why was she bothering to ask so many questions?

After her drink had been refilled and the tavern-keep had moved out of hearing distance, she sat back and looked at Eoghan. He felt very self-conscious.

"Before I say yes, would you answer a few questions for me?"

He nodded.

"Question one: is there really no other skill in your life that you are good at?"

He quickly shook his head.

"Give me honest answers," she warned.

"I... Good at local customs. Good at stew. Spices."

"Question two: have you ever considered working at a tavern instead of killing yourself?"

"Is not family trade."

"Curse your family trade. If you say those words

again, I will immediately walk out of here."

"Sorry." Eoghan considered his answer carefully. "Never knew option was possible."

"I'm sure some tavern-keep out there might appreciate an extra hand. You might find someone who does not have family or children, and who would like to teach another their trade."

"Not question."

She smiled. "Fair point. Question three: would you rather die because you were bad at something instead of living and finding something you are good at? Question four: would you rather give up all that life has to offer just to reclaim an honour that is essentially meaningless? Question five: would you rather have your skin and bones rot in the woods than do what is right for you?"

Her words confused him. Why was she asking so many questions? To go outside of one's family was unheard of in his village, so why would he ever consider a different life? Custom said that it would be best to be dead, not to live and continue to bring shame. He wanted to tell her that he was certain, but a small part of him now wondered if he could find another trade. What if he could work in a tavern and bring mead and stew to weary travellers?

"Question six," she continued, "do you still want me to kill you."

He looked down at his drink and considered his past and present, and all that had been said and done.

He paused.

"Yes."

***

She chose a small clearing just outside the town. It was better for bloodshed, she told him, and there would be no witnesses to misunderstand the situation.

"Payment first," she stated, holding out her hand.

He tossed her a bag of coins. It was all the money he had left.

She held the bag in her hand, testing the weight. "You said it would be a well-paying job."

"Is easy job. Well paid for easy."

She sighed and tucked the bag away. Pulling aside her cloak, she unsheathed a sword from her belt and swung it around, loosening up her wrist. He watched the sharp edge gleam in the sun, and felt a lump form in his throat. Maybe he should have waited for night.

She noticed the hesitation in his face, and stopped swinging her sword.

"You are an idiot," she said.

A mix of hurt and confusion crossed Eoghan's face.

"You do not want to die. You are in love with the idea of an honourable death, but you are too afraid to do it yourself because you are scared to die."

"No," he said, shaking his head fervently. "Want death."

She moved forward and placed her blade against his throat.

"All you need to do is lean forward and turn your head to the right. The blade will cut your throat and you will bleed out and die. If you are so eager to reclaim your honour, do it yourself."

The blade was cold against his throat. It would be so easy for him to do what she had instructed, and yet he remained still.

"No," he said, stepping away from the sword. "Hired you. Will not do job for you."

She rolled her eyes and let the sword rest at her side.

"Fine. If you want to remain an idiot, I will not stop you. Just remember, when you are earthbound, that I gave you multiple chances to back out of this."

He stuck out his chin in an effort to look tough. "No backing out."

"Kneel down and close your eyes."

He took a deep breath, knelt down, and closed his eyes. This was the only way to regain his honour. He was doing the right thing.

She raised the sword high and brought it down.

***

The sky was a bright, vivid blue, with barely a cloud in sight.

Eoghan opened his eyes and took in all the blue. What was this? Was he skyward? He had assumed he would be earthbound because of his dishonour, but that was definitely the sky. There was no blue in earthbound – only darkness and despair until your sentence was fulfilled. Was it possible the pious were wrong?

His head hurt. Was he supposed to feel pain? He knew the customs of life, but not death. There was grass under his hands and he could smell dirt. What was going on?

Eoghan sat up and looked around. He was still in the clearing, although he was now alone. Beside him was his coin bag – the one he had given to the Red-Hand. Opening it, he saw that there were only two pennies left inside.

He was alive. He had no money and was still alive. She must have hit him with the blunt end of the sword, not the blade. Not only had she failed to kill him, but she had taken all his money and disappeared.

What was he supposed to do now? There was no way he would be able to afford another Red-Hand with only two pennies. He would barely be able to afford a meal.

Rising to his feet, he considered his options. He remembered how busy the lowspeak tavern had been during the revels – maybe the tavern-keep could be talked into hiring an extra hand. If so, Eoghan would be able to save his wages, and build up enough to hire another Red-Hand – one who would do the job properly.

Working in a tavern might not pay much, but he was a patient man. Even if it took him years, he would show that Red-Hand that he was not afraid to die.

The Invisible Boy

James was an only child. Sort of. Before he was born, there had been another child -- a brother -- but the child disappeared one night and was never seen again. All that remained was a memory – a shadow.

His parents tried their best to raise him. There was always a roof over his head, clothes on his back, and he never went hungry. They tried their best to love him, but they had given all their love to the other child, and it had disappeared with him.

James grew up hearing stories about his brother, despite his never having reached one year of age. The stories quickly became myths – the perfect child who would have been the perfect son, and the perfect family they could have been. His parents frequently imagined what the child would be like and how he would act if he were here, and compared James to these imaginations. His brother would never disobey his parents or receive low marks on a test. His brother would never raise his voice or fight with the neighbourhood children.

James waited patiently for his parents to forget about his absent brother and love him for who he was, but it never happened. They never forgot about their perfect boy. They continued to talk about how he would have grown up and all that he would have achieved. James knew that he was nothing but a disappointment to his parents. He grew up in the shadow of an invisible boy and he hated every minute of it.

When he was eighteen he decided to leave home. He kept minimal contact with his parents, returning home for holidays or special occasions. Each time he would wonder if his parents had finally moved on, but there would always be some reminder. Another stocking hung along the mantle or an extra place set at the table. Finally, he stopped visiting all together, but still he could not get away from the memories that haunted and mocked him.

One day, he decided that he was going to end this once and for all. He was no longer going to live his life in a shadow, constantly wondering what his perfect brother would have done or how he would have reacted. James was going to become his own person, free from the spirit of a person he had never met. But the only way to do this would be to find this invisible boy and kill him.

James became a traveler. He signed on for work aboard a ship and left the only home he'd ever known. He traveled all over the world, sailing too far off lands. At every port, he would listen for word of his brother, but no word was heard. His task would not be that easy.

Time passed. Whenever James reached a dead end, which was often, he would find another ship and start over again. He changed ships frequently, gaining more and more experience. Over time he moved up in rank, but he never forgot about the fire that burned inside.

Nothing could stand in his way. When the weather grew fierce, he refused to turn back. He would shout at the seas and the skies, and prove that he was no quitter. No matter what the obstacle was, he found a way to get through and persevere. He would never give up, no matter how much time passed or how hopeless it seemed.

One night, many years later, he was sitting in a local

tavern when he heard a name – a very familiar name. A group of men were sitting around a table, drinks clasped in their hands. James turned towards the group and listened as one man recounted a tale of an island that existed, but didn't. It was hidden, and very few people had ever made the journey. Even fewer returned.

The stories said that there was one boy who was able to travel to and from the island with ease. The island was magical and it created a never-ending childhood for this boy and his friends to live in. The boy was brave and strong. The boy was perfect.

Some men laughed at the stories and called them false, but James knew that they were real. He knew that this island existed because of the name the man had said – the name that had haunted him his entire life. The stories said that very few men had been to the island, but James did not let that discourage him. He would go there. He would find this boy and he would destroy him, just as this boy had destroyed his life. It was not fair that his brother lived in a never-ending childhood, while James' childhood had been stolen.

He became a captain and purchased his own ship, hiring a full crew. The journey was mysterious and would not be easy, but he had his men and he had his mission. They sailed for days and nights, letting rumours and legends guide them. James could feel the fire burning strong inside of him. With each day the island was getting closer and closer.

One day he would find this island and he would have his revenge. The boy would suffer for all the wrongs that he had left in his wake.

The boy...

The shadow...

Peter...

Lost Souls

This city was no stranger to lost souls.

People found their way here through determination or dumb luck. They found their way here because this was where they belonged. Although there were many different circumstances that guided them on this path, at the core their stories were the same. They were lost souls looking for a home.

This city, with its winding streets and strange directions, where in order to go right you must first go left. Where nothing seems to make sense, except that it feels like home.

They were out there, in the night, drinking and dancing and having fun. In this city they didn't have to worry about being anyone else. Here they could relax and be their true selves.

But little did they know – once they arrived, they could never leave. This city had trapped them, and would hold them until the day they died. Most would never realize this. The idea of leaving would never cross their minds.

But she knew. She knew everything.

They couldn't see her, but she watched each and every one of them. She had built this city. She was their king, their queen, their overlord. She was the one who kept them here, feeding on the energy that radiated from their souls.

And she was ravenous.

The Search

She could hear water flowing nearby. Opening her eyes, Elise realized that she was sitting in the forest, among flowers as white as her hair. She couldn't remember why she was here or why everything felt familiar.

The sky had grown dark but the lantern provided enough light to search by. Suddenly she remembered everything – she was looking for her sister, who'd disappeared while playing near the woods. Elise quickly rose to her feet. She'd only meant to rest for a second but must have nodded off. These woods were full of strange experiences and dangerous creatures, and everyone knew to avoid it after dark. She thought about turning back. Maybe her sister had returned home. Maybe everything was fine.

A noise on the other side of the stream caught her attention. It sounded like someone crying. Calling out her sister's name, Elise walked towards the stream, lantern raised high. The water flowed perilously, washing over large stones indicating the treacherous path across. She hesitated, but the crying grew louder and she knew she had to move forward.

When she was halfway across the stream, a shriek pierced the air, startling her. Her foot slipped, and letting out a panicked cry, Elise fell. Cold water rushed over her, soaking her dress and pulling her down into impossible, unknowable depths.

Everything went black.

She could hear water flowing nearby. Opening her eyes, Elise realized that she was sitting in the forest, among flowers as white as her hair.

A Powerful Magic

Although she couldn't hear her heart pounding in her chest, she could feel it. As sunrise drew closer, a dreadful feeling washed over her. She was running out of time.

Standing in the doorway of her cottage, a thick blanket wrapped around her shoulders, she looked out across the open field. He'd said he would return, but what if something terrible had happened? What if he'd been injured, or worse…?

As the sky began to lighten, her heart beat faster. She pulled the blanket tighter, but it couldn't combat the icy chill that was slowly spreading throughout her body. Suddenly her eyes widened. There he was – racing towards her, a red glass bottle held tightly in his hand. She wanted to run to him, but the invisible barrier that kept her prisoner inside the cottage held her back. Tears filled her eyes. He wasn't going to make it.

He was ten feet away when the sun broke free of the horizon. A cold hand gripped her heart and her breath caught in her throat. The blanket dropped from her shoulders, her eyes closed, and she fell.

* * *

He tried desperately to wake her, but the curse had taken hold. No breath escaped her mouth and her skin was cold to the touch.

Cradling her head gently in his lap, he uncorked the bottle and held it to her lips, praying the potion would still work, praying that she would come back to him...

Green Scales

It was the strangest sensation.

Where once her legs had been there was now a glittering, gleaming, green tail.

When the cave witch told her the price, she'd almost laughed out loud. Her voice? Really? She'd never liked the way it sounded, all high-pitched and squeaky, so she was more than prepared to give up her voice for a tail.

She'd been sceptical of the elixir contained within the small glass bottle, especially because it tasted like ordinary salt water, but as she walked into the ocean she could feel the magic starting to work. In less than a minute the elixir had done its job, and the bright green scales of her new tail were shimmering in the sunlight. She was almost afraid to touch them, as if they'd disappear as soon as they came in contact with her skin.

She flicked her new tail tentatively, feeling the muscles of her former legs working together. A smile broke out on her face as one quick flick propelled droplets of water into the air, catching the sunlight as they arced.

Turning to the water, her smile widened. It was time for an adventure.

Tenebris

She lived in darkness. Her world was one of touch, taste, sound, and smell. Her world was all she knew.

Until one day she overheard a story, a story told in a whisper, the voice so low she had to stop breathing to hear it. It told of how she'd once lived in the light, surrounded by brilliant colours and shapes, and how she'd been taken from that world and placed in the dark.

"But why?" she asked softly.

"I do not know," was the reply.

She tried to remember a world of light and colour, but it eluded her. Was the story true? Did that other world exist? Curiosity filled her and one night she dared to ask:

"How do I find the light?"

The reply floated to her like a soft breeze, carrying instructions on how to find the veil and what to do once she arrived.

Travelling through the darkness, she hoped she'd not gone mad, but it wasn't until she reached a room she'd never known existed and placed her hand upon an unfamiliar wall that she knew the story was true.

The wall was sturdy but soft and smelled strangely familiar. Reaching down, she grabbed a handful of stones before pulling her arm back to throw them. When they hit the wall they broke through, revealing points of blinding light. Raising an arm to shield her unaccustomed eyes, she felt the brightness pushing away the darkness clouding her memory, revealing the truth.

The Price of Beauty

It was worth the pain.

The birds were such small, delicate creatures, landing on her outstretched hands with only the gentlest of touches. At times she felt like a fairy princess, gathering woodland creatures about her, but it only took a matter of seconds for that illusion to be shattered. Their small feet would tighten around her fingers, claws digging into her skin as the birds steadied themselves. She felt it all—the sharpness as their talons sunk in, the slight relief that came as her soft flesh finally broke under the pressure, and the warm blood that ran down her hands, dropping onto the ground below. Yet she did not move or discourage the birds in any way.

The pain was a small price to pay. Once settled, the birds sang so sweetly and beautifully that she couldn't bear to disturb them. She stayed as still as possible, letting the music block out the hurt in her fingers and the smell of her own blood in the air.

She stayed until the birds tired and flew away. Afterwards, she would clean her bloody hands and wrap her wounds, but all the while she would hum their melodies to herself.

It was worth the pain to hear such beautiful music.

The Guide

In the dead of night, go to the darkest part of the forest. She will be waiting.

When you've arrived, she will start to walk. Follow. Let her torch be your guide, like a beacon in the darkness.

Do not stray from the path. Do not fall behind. Do not take your eyes off the fire. Those who become lost will never be found and will wander the forest forever, searching for a light to lead them home.

Do not ask where you are going. She will not answer. Hold your tongue. If you vex her, she will lead you astray. It is safer to be silent.

Be sure that you are kind of heart. Those who walk this path for ill reasons will find only disappointment. Those who have pure intentions will be rewarded. She knows which one you are.

The way is long, but worth the travel. Do not complain. Do not rest. Do not give up hope.

If you have followed the rules, eventually you will find it. She will stop, and before your very eyes the path will open, revealing what it is you seek.

What you do next is up to you.

The Blight

She was princess to a dying throne.

The Forest Kingdom was coming to an end: its verdant grass turned a dull brown, vibrantly colored flowers had faded, and trees that stood tall and strong withered. Nobody knew what caused the blight or how to fight it. They'd performed numerous protection rituals and failed every time. There was no stopping death.

Her family had resigned themselves, but she couldn't stand still and watch her forest die. Wandering the lands, she felt her kingdom's pain crying out. Coming upon a glade where she'd spent many hours, her heart ached at the dried grass and wilted trees. Kneeling among a shriveled patch of marigolds, she prayed that her forest could be saved. Sorrowful tears filled her eyes, spilling down her cheeks.

Looking down, she saw that where her tears had landed the brilliant color returned to the flowers. Her heart leapt with joy, before quickly falling. Could she cry enough for the entire kingdom?

Suddenly, she knew what to do.

The cut did not hurt at first, but then the pain blossomed, spreading throughout her body. Steeling herself, she kept the blade steady and continued. After a few careful slices, she finally held her heart in her hands.

Burying her heart beneath the willow tree, she knew that its strength would help the forest battle this terrible blight and come back to its former glory. Her body would die but her spirit would live on, protecting her kingdom forever.

Le Trou de Lapin

Calie never would have discovered Café Wünder if it hadn't been for the woman in white. She'd been walking down the street, wondering what to have for dinner that night, when she suddenly noticed a tall woman in an immaculate white tuxedo, white top hat, and cane. The outfit was so incredibly out of place that she couldn't help staring. Nobody else seemed to notice the woman – who was walking with an oblivious smile on her face – yet everyone seemed to instinctively move out of her way. Calie watched the woman pause and take a round silver watch out of her suit pocket. As she opened it and looked at the time her expression changed to one of surprise and she quickly shoved it back into her pocket before picking up her pace. A glint of sunlight brought Calie's attention to the watch falling out of the woman's pocket, but before she could say anything, the woman turned and disappeared.

Hurrying over to the watch, Calie picked it up and looked around for the woman. She wondered if she had somehow managed to walk through a brick wall, but then she saw a small gap between buildings – a gap that she'd never noticed before. It was barely big enough for a person to walk through, but after squeezing into it, it opened up into a larger alleyway. Red bricks lined the walls of the alley, the shade somehow growing brighter towards the end, and the ground was made of cobblestones of various shapes, sizes, and colours. Looking to her left, she saw a street sign written in cursive proclaiming this to be 'Le Trou de Lapin'. Everything about the alley looked out of place, as if it had been plucked from someone's imagination and dropped into the real world.

Once she was over her initial shock, Calie noticed that the woman in the tuxedo had reached the end of the alley and was opening a small white door on the back wall. She had to bend almost double to fit through, but did so with practised ease, slipping inside.

Calie stared at the white door before looking down at the pocket watch in her hand. There was something about the alley that unnerved her, like stepping from reality into a dream. She could easily put the watch on the ground and turn back, or go home and post an ad in the newspaper. Calie liked knowing things and being in control of her surroundings, and it would make perfect sense for her to turn away and step back into reality. Except... Except how often is a person presented with the opportunity to discover something completely new? If she walked away then there was a very real chance that she'd never be able to find this alley ever again, and that the mystery of it would sit in the back of her mind, causing her to wonder forever.

Closing her hand around the watch, she knew she had to go through the door.

As she drew closer she saw a sign that read 'Café Wünder'. Each letter was in a different script, size, and colour. It was possible that behind this door was a perfectly normal café, but Calie doubted it. Taking a deep breath, she reached out and opened the door. Even though she was at least a foot shorter than the tuxedo woman, she still had to duck to fit through the doorframe.

Inside, the cafe appeared to be a quaint English tea room. There were visible wooden beams, pastel walls, white linens on the tables, and more lace than she'd seen in her entire life. All of the wrought iron tables were empty except for one, where two men sat, both wearing jeans, white t-shirts, black vests, and top hats. They were sipping tea from china cups patterned with flowers and edged in gold, and on the table between them was a 3-tired silver tray with bite-sized treats.

To the left was a long counter. Standing behind it was a young man wearing a purple velvet coat and a black top hat, with a smile so wide that you could probably see it from space. The name-tag on his coat proclaimed that his name was Wellesley.

"How may I help you?" he asked as Calie moved closer to the counter.

She was so busy taking in her surroundings that for a moment she almost forgot her purpose. Holding out her hand, she presented Wellesley with the pocket watch. "One of your customers – I mean, I'm not sure if she's a customer or if she works here, or even if she owns the place, but she just came in a few minutes before me." She paused, realizing that the tall women was nowhere in sight, despite having entered not that long ago. "Sorry," she started again. "I found this watch, and the woman who owns it came in here."

Wellesley put his hand out and she handed it to him. He looked at it thoughtfully, and a few seconds later the large smile re-appeared. "Ah, yes. She's always losing things. I'll be sure to give it to her."

"Um, good. That's great." Calie paused. Now that her good deed was completed, should she order something? Should she leave? Was this the end of her adventure? Coming out of her thoughts, she noticed that Wellesley's eyes had narrowed slightly, as if he was trying to get a read on her, but before she could say anything, he spoke.

"We usually give a reward to anyone kind enough to

return lost items," he smiled. "Tea and a scone. It's not much, but a kind gesture deserves one in return, yes?" His smile widened. "What can I get for you?"

Calie looked up at the menu on the wall, which had been divided into 2 sections: DRINK ME and EAT ME. She quickly scanned through the options, which were a variety of teas, scones, and desserts. "I'll try the lapsang souchong tea and..." she looked over the scones, trying to figure out which one sounded the most appetizing.

"Might I suggest the maple-brown-sugar scone?" Wellesley piped up. "They pair quite well together."

She nodded. "Sounds great."

"Excellent!" He disappeared through a set of bright blue swinging doors for a few seconds before reappearing with a cup of tea in fine china and a scone cut into eight small pieces on a matching plate. "Since it's your first time here, I'd recommend Room 4. It has a beautiful view of the garden."

She nodded again and followed Wellesley up the stairs and down a hallway lined with multi-coloured doors, numbered in no obvious pattern. He led her to a dark blue door numbered with an orange 4.

"I hope you enjoy," he said, placing her tea and scone on the table inside. "And remember, when one is partaking in high tea, it is best to take dainty sips and tiny bites," he cautioned, before closing the door and leaving her alone in the room.

Callie took in her new surroundings. She had no idea what was going on with this place or why she wasn't at one of the tables downstairs, but there wasn't anything in the room that seemed dangerous. The door opened easily enough, so she wasn't trapped. The walls were painted sky blue with white trim, and there was a large window at the back wall, with a chair and table in front of it. Through the window she could see a beautiful view of a garden, with every kind of flower imaginable. She had no idea that such a garden existed in this city.

Sitting down at the table, she picked up a piece of scone to pop in her mouth when she suddenly recalled Wellesley's words. They sounded like a warning and something that should be heeded. Carefully regarding the food in her hand, she tentatively took a small bite. There was nothing unusual about the taste – maple and brown sugar, just the right amount of crumble, and lighter than expected. In fact, it was quite delicious. When she finished, she thought about taking another bite but stopped herself. There was a nagging feeling in the back of her mind that something was really strange about this place. Maybe it was something Wellesley did with all new customers, some kind of initiation joke, or maybe it was something more. Whatever it night be, she felt the need to be cautious.

A few more seconds passed and she still felt normal. She reached out for the scone again, but as her hand moved towards the plate she noticed that the table was getting bigger. In fact, the whole room was growing.

When it finally stopped, she looked around the room and realized that it hadn't gotten bigger – she had gotten smaller. Looking around, she estimated that she was half a foot shorter and yet still in proportion. Was it the scone? How could food do something like this? What kind of cafe had she stumbled across? Something clicked in her brain and she took a small sip of tea and waited. After a few seconds she was her normal size again. Calie couldn't help laughing out out loud. It was ridiculous and impossible, and the most amazing thing she'd ever experienced. This place was incredible.

Examining the room more closely, she noticed small ladders attached to the table and chairs. It made sense – it wouldn't be good for a person to shrink down and not be able to get to their tea. Now that she knew what was going on, she spent the next hour shrinking and growing, exploring how much of a bite or a sip would change her. It had been exhilarating to grow so tall and then to suddenly be so short. It should have been impossible, but unless the food was spiked with some kind of strange drug, it was happening. And to think that she'd almost walked away.

She had just finished her last bite of scone, which took her back down to her regular height, when there was a knock on the door.

"How's everything going in there?" Wellesley's voice asked.

"Great," she answered.

The door opened and Wellesley entered. When he looked at her, his eyes widened in surprise and his smile increased.

"I must say, it's rare to see a first-timer show so much restraint. I'm impressed."

"No, I'm the one who's impressed. I hope that I'll be able to find this place again."

His eyes twinkled. "I'm sure you will."

***

Over the next week, Calie went back to the café four times, and every time Wellesley would be wearing a different name tag. The first couple of times she wondered if maybe he was a twin or triplet, but then she realized that it was always Wellesley. She never thought to question the different name tags or ask for his true name. Everything about the café was strange and wonderful, and Calie didn't want to do anything to upset the magic. She never told anyone else about it, partly because she wanted it to be her little secret, but also because she doubted that anyone would believe her.

During her visits she tried different foods and teas,

learning what each one did. Some were stronger than others, causing her to grow and shrink much much and much faster. The cafe even had a few items that were merely normal food and did nothing other than taste delicious.

She took meticulous notes in a small notepad that was in her purse, along with multiple containers that arrived empty and left full. She was worried that Wellesley would ask to see inside her purse, but he never did. Every time she left, he gave her a trusting smile that started to weigh on her conscience.

***

A few days later, Calie was at the local museum, taking in a new gallery exhibit. The pieces were on loan from a private owner, showcasing famous abstract paintings. There were pieces by Pollock, Mondrian, Rothko, but the centrepiece was a painting by Kandinsky that was surrounded by controversy. A family claimed that it was theirs and that it had been stolen during World War 2, but so many records had been destroyed during that time and they had no way to prove ownership. The current owner swore that they had purchased it legally before World War 2, but refused to prove it because there was no point in 'digging out that dusty old document'. All the controversy served to make the painting more intriguing and it was the most important and expensive painting the museum had ever housed.

It was getting close to closing time as Calie finished wandering through the exhibit. Tiny bells sounded, letting the public know that there was only ten minutes left. Giving the room one last look, she moved towards the bathroom. In one of the stalls, she opened her purse and took out a container with a piece of scone marked with a 'B'. Slipping the scone into her pocket, she left the bathroom and headed for the stairwell, where she knew there were no security cameras. The stairs were empty, so she quickly took the scone out and ate it all, shrinking down to the size of a bug.

Taking a deep breath, she moved to a dark corner and waited. She'd done her research and knew that it took about half and hour for security to walk through and confirm that the building was empty. At night there were two security guards, but they stayed in the security office, since the building had its own tech. There were laser grids, doors with bars, and cameras on all the artwork. It was a high-tech security system, but one thing they didn't plan for was a way to protect against a thief who could shrink down to the size of an ant.

After forty-five minutes, she ducked under the stairwell door and made her way to the Kandinsky's room, which took a lot longer with her tiny legs. There was a moment of panic when she realized that she was too short to get over the bottom of the barred door that had come down to protect the room, but the tiniest sip of tea solved that problem. Luckily she was still small enough to walk underneath the floor lasers, although she ducked her head instinctively. Eventually she made it to the wall where the painting was hanging.

Now it was time for the scary part. There was no way for her to get the painting without setting off the lasers, so she was going to have be very quick and very careful. She was wearing a black bodysuit underneath her clothes, so she took off her shirt and pants and stuffed them into her purse. Then she took out a black ballaclava and put it on, being careful to hide her hair. Next she took out a container and a thermos, both marked with an '8'. Putting her purse on the floor, she held the scone in her left hand before drinking the contents of the thermos, tossing the empty container to the side. She shot up to eight feet tall, breaking the laser grid and setting off the alarms. Grabbing the Kandinsky off the wall with her right hand set off even more alarms, so she quickly swallowed the scone, shrinking herself and the painting down to her previous size. There was nothing she could do about the security tapes, but hopefully they would show a masked eight foot tall person suddenly appearing and disappearing, which should confuse the heck out of the police.

The noise from the alarms was deafening, but Calie knew that she had to keep going. She grabbed her purse and quickly made her way to the door, hugging the wall. Security arrived before she made it out of the room, so although she had to be careful not to get stepped on, at least she didn't have to climb over the door again.

The escape route had to change slightly, with all the activity going on and all the police in the gallery, but she managed to make it out of the museum before sunrise. By the time she reached a safe place to grow back to her normal height, she was exhausted. She took off the mask, put her shirt and pants back on, and took a careful sip from from a thermos marked 'N'. She grew to one foot tall, at which point she put the painting aside before drinking the rest of the tea, returning to her normal height. Then she carefully picked up the tiny painting and put it in her pocket. At home she could grow it back to normal size, but for now it was the perfect size to carry without anyone noticing. The ordeal was finally over, and she was exhausted but successful.

***

When she returned to the café a week later, Wellesley greeted her with his familiar smile and a name-tag reading 'Gloucester'. "Haven't seen you here for a while," he remarked. "I was almost worried."

"Had to make an emergency trip," she replied. "Family thing."

He nodded. "You must have missed all the excitement. A certain painting was stolen from the gallery last week."

"Oh, really?" she asked, feigning surprise.

"Yes. The famous Kandinsky. The police say that the robber suddenly appeared out of thin air, took the painting, and disappeared. Really strange."

"Wow. That's insane." Although she continued to pretend, something about the way he was speaking was starting to make her nervous. Did he suspect that she had something to do with the robbery? Would he turn her in? Would he ban her from the cafe?

"I also heard, through one of my grapevines, that a certain painting has made its way to a certain, very deserving, family. Call me strange, but there are occasions where I feel that the end justifies the means."

She couldn't help smiling. "Me too," she nodded.

Wellesley's smile grew wider. "So, what may I get for you today?"

She made her order and paid, and as Wellesley handed over her items he gestured for her to lean in close.

"I read about a really great exhibit coming next week to the museum. A famous gem that's just as disputed as the Kandinsky was. The article is in Room 12, if you care to read about it."

Then he winked at her before disappearing through the bright blue swinging doors.

Calie smiled and headed for Room 12.

Jyaan's Magical Curiosities and Stalwart Advice

Jyaan prided herself on providing exceptional customer service, but even she had to admit that it was quite the challenge to stay pleasant while a broadsword was pointed at her face. Luckily, she'd had practice. This wasn't the first time a weapon had been directed her way and she sadly doubted that it would be the last. Such was the life of a mystical shop owner.

The person wielding the sword was a Djal warrior. Their kind were known for their viciousness, and it was said that a Djal baby would stab you if there was a knife within reach. Jyaan had nearly had a heart attack when the warrior burst through the portal door for the world of Djaloom, her sword ready and anger radiating off her in waves.

"You said that the gemstone key would open the Great Stone Door," the warrior growled. Her voice resonated throughout the small shop, reverberating along the wooden walls. Jyaan was thankful that her stock was kept in the back, as she was certain the warrior's anger was fierce enough to cause even the sturdiest shelving unit to crumble in fear.

Attempting to ignore the sharp point mere inches from her face, Jyaan put on her best smile.

"Well," she began gently, "my exact words *might* have been that the gemstone key would open the door *if* it still held a charge within it, and then I think I rambled on a bit about how it's *impossible* to tell if the charge has been used or not, but let's not dwell on that! Let's move ahead to the part where I said I'd give you a full refund if it didn't work, okay?"

It was a gamble to bring up their last interaction, but Jyaan was hoping that the magical words 'Full Refund' would placate any irritability. Most customers only remembered what they wanted to remember, and the Djal were no different. They were so focused on their quests that they refused to consider the possibility that something might actually go wrong. If such a misfortune befell them, they were quick to blame anyone but themselves, including innocent shop owners who had definitely mentioned the fine print.

"The gemstones are very fickle creatures and regrettably that was my last one," Jyaan said, trying hard to maintain her pleasant tone. "But perhaps it's possible to open the door through other means. Can you think of any such way?"

Her optimism had the desired effect and the grumbling quieted as the warrior considered the question. The sword unconsciously lowered as she thought, until it was almost pointing at the floor. Jyaan knew better than to breathe a sigh of relief too soon, but she did relish the small victory.

"There is a tale of a stone spirit that lives in the quarry to the East," the warrior said slowly as she tried to bring the memory forth. "If you displease the spirit then you will be cursed for all time, but if you appease her, she will gift you a gemstone key." She shook her head. "But it is merely a child's tale, told for amusement."

"Tales have to start from something!" Jyaan smiled broadly, finally seeing a light at the end of the tunnel.

"Now, what do you need to appease the stone spirit? Wealth? Craftsmanship? Cilantro?"

The warrior seemed hesitant, but after a pause she spoke. *"Shades of green will bring much silence, shades of red will bring the blood, shades of grey will hold the violence, and shades of blue will part the mud. Precious items bring a thrill, large and heavy block the way, pebbles in a pond shall still, and glowing lights may call the fray."*

"Excellent!" Jyaan exclaimed, thumping her fist on the well-worn counter that separated her from the warrior. "I have just the thing! Wait here while I go in the back to retrieve it!"

She hurried into her back room, shutting the door behind her and leaning against it with a large sigh. What she'd said was a complete lie—the riddle made no sense to her—but at least she was further away from the broadsword.

A small part of her considered grabbing the nearest trinket, hustling the warrior out of her shop, and closing the portal to Djaloom once and for all, but she couldn't risk losing the patronage of the stone druids who resided in those mountains. Adventurers from the worlds of Sylvaain and Traivelle depended on those wares, and she'd hate to disappoint customers who'd never once threatened her.

Tapping her index finger on her forehead, she willed herself to unravel the riddle. It was ridiculous, as most children's rhymes were, but there had to be some truth to it. Although it was strange for a spirit to reside in mud, it sounded better than silence and safer than blood. The riddle said 'shades' so she should have at least three different kinds of blue to call the spirit. Putting a stop to violence sounded handy, so she should include some grey, just in case.

The second part required more thought. After a process of elimination, Jyaan surmised that it would be best to thrill the spirit with precious items. She definitely didn't want to block the way, and although she didn't know the context of 'fray', it didn't sound good. Stillness could be useful in certain situations, so pebbles would be a good backup.

Having unraveled the riddle to satisfaction, Jyaan jumped into action, scouring the shelves for the items required. To the untrained eye the back room was a vast jumble of magical items, with summoning scrolls next to craven images, above jars of chocolate-walnut cookies, but to Jyaan everything had a particular place and purpose. Sometime she forgot what certain things were, but it never took her too long to find any item she required. In record time she had three small bags prepared.

Opening the door a crack, she looked out to see what her customer was doing. Relief washed over her when she saw the warrior waiting calmly. There was a hint of impatience in the way she tapped her armoured foot on the wooden floor, but it was better than a sword in the face.

"Success!" Jyaan said cheerfully, walking back out to the counter. "Now, if all goes well, you'll only need this bag," she held up a small leather bag with a '1' written on it, which contained six blue gems of differing hues. "This is marked with a one because it's the first bag you should try. If the riddle is right, these blue gems will call and thrill the spirit, and hopefully that will be enough to get the gemstone key."

She held up a bag with a white cross marked on it. "This bag contains grey pebbles, so if things go wrong, use this to bring a whole lot of stillness. I'm not sure what kind of stillness, but hopefully the good, helpful kind. Are you following?"

The warrior nodded.

"Now, this final bag," Jyaan held up the bag with a blue circle on it. "This contains blue pebbles and is your back-up. This should call and hold the spirit, and hopefully buy you enough time to bargain for the key. Got it?"

The warrior paused to think. "How much?"

"If we consider the refund on the gemstone key, it'll cost you five silver for all three bags."

"Deal!" The warrior reached into her satchel, pulled out a round purple gem the size of her palm, and placed it on the table. Five silver coins quickly followed.

Jyaan held out the three bags, which the warrior took and carefully tucked away.

"Good luck in your quest!" Jyaan said cheerfully. "And if this doesn't work out, we'll try something new! Remember my motto—There's Always Hope!"

Keeping the bright smile on her face, Jyaan watched the warrior head towards the back wall. She passed by doors of all shapes, sizes, and materials, each containing portals to different worlds, until reaching a tall stone door to Djaloom. She walked through the portal, instantly transporting herself back to her world. Once she was gone, Jyaan let out a huge sigh of relief.

After a brief recovery period, she pulled out a large leather-bound book and a quill. She made a few inventory notes before turning to the calendar in the back and marking down a prediction for when the Djal warrior might return. If the bags did their job then she wouldn't see the warrior for many moons, but if there was even the slightest chance that the angry broadsword would return, Jyaan wanted to give her future self some advance notice.

Putting the book and quill away, she headed to the back room to get herself a chocolate-walnut cookie. She'd definitely earned it.

Family Secrets

The ocean called to her constantly. Some days she would spend hours sitting on the beach and staring out at the water, watching the waves push up on the shore before falling back. The mood of the water depended on the weather and sometimes, if she sat for long enough, she would see many different kinds of waves—from soft and gentle to rough and ragged, and everything in between. Nature was always changing, always moving on. Unlike her.

There were others who stared at the ocean, but they were usually older men, retired sailors who used to spend their days out on the water but had grown too old for that life. They stayed close to the wharfs, where they could watch boats filled with younger men shove off and sail away. There wasn't much else for them to do in the tiny town on the northern tip of Newfoundland.

Despite all her hours spent staring at the ocean, she never looked at the boats. Her eyes were always on the water.

***

She met her husband at the beach. It was a beautiful summer day, but she was sitting on a rock, crying. Although they were complete strangers, he walked over to her and tried to make her smile. The overwhelming grief she was feeling rendered her unable to respond, and when he realized this he stopped talking and sat with her, silently.

Later, after she had no more tears to shed, he took her into town, bought her a hot meal, and they began to warm up to one another. She told him that she'd been out on the water and had lost her way. She was stranded on this strange beach, with no idea where she was or how to get back to her home. He inquired if she was from somewhere else in Newfoundland or if she was from Labrador, but there was no response. He tried to ask for more details, but she refused to speak and eventually he let it go. When she finished her meal, he offered her a place to stay at his house for as long as she needed. Her sorrow had touched him and he offered to sleep on the couch and provide for her until she could find her way home. As she had nowhere else to go she had to accept.

In the following days she went back to the beach, spending hours searching for her salvation, but every night she came back unsuccessful. He never went with her or asked what she was doing, and she never told him. If he ever saw her crying, he would sit silently with her, offering company without words.

As the days turned into weeks, her hope began to decline. One day, when he came home from hunting, he found her curled up on the bed, sobbing deeply and talking incoherently about how she would never see her home again. He sat next to her, placing a comforting hand on her shoulder.

Shortly after they were married.

She tried to be a good wife, learning how to cook and clean, but still she felt the pull of the ocean. Some days she would leave half-kneaded bread on the counter and wander out to the beach, standing near the water. As much as she wanted to run in and feel the waves rolling around her, she was unable to leave the beach. All she could do was stand and watch and try not to cry.

Whenever her husband found her standing there, sorrow would cross his brow. And as he gently put an arm around her and led her home, he would say nothing.

***

She never told him the truth because she didn't think he would understand. It was easier to keep it deep within her, buried under all the grief and sadness. It was easier to try not to think about it.

The truth was something he would never believe. Humans were generally unable to understand anything that was out of the ordinary, and she was far from ordinary. She was a creature of the ocean, born in the water, spending days with her family and friends frolicking in the waves and traveling along the ocean currents. Unfortunately she had a dangerous desire. She loved to go on land and travel to small towns, stealing clothing along the way, so that she could observe the locals living their everyday life. Her family warned her with stories of many others of their kind who had walked onto land never to return, but she did not heed their tales.

On the day she walked out of the ocean for the last time, she ventured onto this strange land, shedding her seal skin to become human. Her skin had been carefully hidden away, but when she returned to the beach it was no longer there.

Without her skin, she could never return to her true form or to her family and friends. They remained nearby for days, waiting for her to return, but eventually they had to move on. As much as she wanted to join them, she could not. Her skin was long gone, stolen by someone who may or may not have known its worth. Perhaps it had been crafted into a coat and was now worn by a woman who marvelled at its softness and warmth.

Although her husband had shown her great kindness during her time of need, she could not bring herself to tell him the truth. What if he thought she was crazy? What if he decided to leave her? Would telling him the truth result in anything positive?

No. Some secrets were better left unsaid.

***

Some days her husband brought up the subject of children, but she did not want any. She feared that they would also feel the pull of the ocean, yearning to be one with the water, unable to feel whole. Or maybe she was fearful that they would be born with a skin and take to the waters, doing what she could no longer do, leaving her behind.

Although he tried to hide his disappointment, she knew that he yearned to be a father. Since she could not give him that, she resolved instead to be the best wife. While he hunted in the woods, she cooked and cleaned and mended his clothing.

One day, she was cleaning the bedroom when her bucket of water caught on the edge of the trunk at the foot of their bed. As she watched the water spill over the top of the trunk, falling in between the gaps in the wood, her eyes widened and her heart began to race. She had never before opened this trunk, not in all the years of their marriage. Just as her secrets were locked inside of her, her husband kept his secrets inside this trunk, and as curious as she was about what was inside, she knew that she could never ask. Until she was comfortable sharing her truth, she had no right to ask about his.

But if she didn't open the trunk the water would destroy everything inside, and the longer she hesitated, the worse the water damage would. Her husband was in the woods and wouldn't return home until after dark, so the decision was hers alone. Letting out a resolved sigh, she realized that the time had finally come. If she opened this trunk, she would also need to open up her past. When her husband walked through the door, she would have to tell him ev¬erything. It was time.

Prying open the trunk, she lifted the lid and saw a handmade quilt lying on top. Removing it, she tried to shake off the water before hanging it over the side of their bed to dry. It was not as soft as their current quilt, with squares of odd, un-matched fabrics, but it looked warm enough. It must have been made by his mother or someone else whose memory he held dear. Why he left it in the trunk, she did not know, but maybe it was too precious for everyday use.

Underneath the quilt was a man's jacket, made of small squares of soft brown fur, probably rabbit. She lifted it from the trunk, checking to see if any water had gotten on it, but as it moved her eye fell on what had been underneath, her breath quickly caught in her throat and the coat fell to the floor. As her trembling hand touched the dark grey fur she felt a warmth wash over her – a feeling she had not experienced for years.

Tears filled her eyes and she pulled the seal skin close, hugging it to her body. She was so relieved at its appearance that it was ten minutes before she realized what it meant.

Her husband had it all along. He was the person who had stolen it from the beach, who had hidden it under her very nose in an unlocked trunk for years. She'd thought that he was respecting her secrets but the truth was that he knew everything about her. He had known all along about her true form. He had watched her mourn her family and friends, crying for the life she would never have, while her salvation rested mere feet away.

In all her years she had never imagined that her skin would be under the same roof. She had never thought that her husband would be so cruel.

When she walked away from the house for what would be the final time, she left no note. The jacket and quilt had been placed inside the trunk, in their usual place, and the lid had been closed. When her husband returned home from hunting he would find everything just as he'd left it.

The only clue she left behind was her wedding ring, taking the place of her fur. Perhaps, once he realized that she was truly gone, he would open the trunk and find the ring and realize what it meant.

How would he would react? Would it be anger? Fear? Quiet acceptance?

The truth was that she no longer cared.

She strode to the beach, her fur clasped tightly in her arms. Kicking off her shoes, she walked into the water for the first time in years. The cold ocean water swirled against her legs.

It felt like home.

Left Behind

The news arrived at noon and shortly thereafter Susan's whole world came crashing down. She'd never particularly liked having siblings – especially when she could tell that her parents favored them above her – but she'd never *not* wanted them. And despite the lacking attention, she'd always loved her mum and dad. The divide that had opened up between them over the years was not enough to break the fact that they were family.

And yet… In one terrible, horrible instant, she was all that was left, and for the first time in her life, she was truly alone.

The funeral had been hard on her: so many caskets for one service. She sat alone, too overcome with grief to say anything. Smiling faces looked out at her from the photographs atop each casket, but instead of remembering how happy they had once been all she could see was how they mocked her still. *'We're happy'*, the faces seemed to say, *'happy and at peace. It's only you now, all alone and miserable.'*

After that day she grew more solitary, spending most of her time in her small apartment, surrounded by books. Although she had many suitors, they never lasted long and she never married. It was hard for her to talk to other people. Nobody else had gone through what she'd experienced or knew her kind of suffering. Some days she longed for death, for an end to it all – she wanted so desperately to see her family again, to hear their voices and be at their sides once more – but that decision wasn't hers to make. She knew that when it was her time it would happen, and so she went on with her life.

When the day finally came she found herself being pulled into a light that was golden and bright. She landed in a large green garden, with tall grass and flowers, and a bright blue sky above. A smile quickly crossed her face and she looked around for her family, but they weren't there. Instead, it was Him.

"Is my family here?" she asked politely, trying not to stare at his large white teeth.

He motioned with his head for her to look to the right.

Suddenly she noticed the large sheet of glass beside her that stretched from the ground to the sky and seemed to go on forever. She'd have sworn that it hadn't been there before but now it was obvious. Walking closer to it, she put her hands on the glass and looked through. There they were, on the other side. Her family, together, laughing and having a grand old time, unaware that she was watching.

"This land is no longer for you," He said with a growl.

She remembered enough to be afraid of the beast's words. This was His land and He had absolute power over it. Anything that happened here was by His decree and there was no arguing. At least, not for her.

It was He, so long ago, who had cursed her with being left behind. *'You are too old to come back,'* He'd said to her before she left his land, *'forget all of this and live a normal life.'*

She tried to protest but his mighty growl overpowered her words and scared the fight from her.

Back home she'd wanted so desperately to remember and reminisce like her brothers and sisters, but the beast's words echoed in her head, taking over her memories and forcing her to think of other things. While her siblings chatted non-stop about their grand adventures, she remained silent. There was nothing for her but a sense of emptiness where there should have been fondness, and a lion's roar damming her to a life separate from those she had been so close to.

Thinking that she had done something to dissatisfy Him, she tried to obey His words and live like a normal English girl, but her actions caused a rift between her and her siblings. They couldn't understand why she wouldn't join them in their talks of the old days and she had no words to explain.

She'd thought that in the end He would forgive her and let her come back, but now she could see that He had other ideas.

"You said the same words to Peter when we left," she said carefully, hiding her anger. "Why is he allowed to be with them?"

"Peter has proven himself to be worthy. You have done nothing but cause trouble. I have no patience for your type."

"But what about Lucy? You always seemed delighted by her."

"Lucy is very different from you."

"Then why did you bring me there in the first place?" she asked, nearly in tears. "Why show me such joy and happiness and then take it all away? Why?"

"I was in need of two sons and two daughters," He

said. "Had there been another daughter of Eve, I would gladly have left you behind." The large golden lion turned around and began walking away from her.

"Wait!" she cried. "Why can I not join them? Haven't I suffered enough?"

He ignored her and disappeared into the distance.

She ran to the glass that separated her from her loved ones and beat it with her fists, but it did not break. Nobody on the other side could hear or see her. Her fists pounded the glass until tears streaked her face and there was no energy left in her.

"All I wanted was to return one day," she sobbed to herself, collapsing to the ground. "All I wanted was to be with them again." She put her head in her hands and wept. How had such an innocent and magical adventure become so tainted? Why was her life the only one filled with torment and injustice?

Sobbing, she did not see the lion appear on the other side of the glass. He walked towards her friends and family with a gentle smile on his face and within seconds everyone she had ever loved could no longer remember the name Susan.

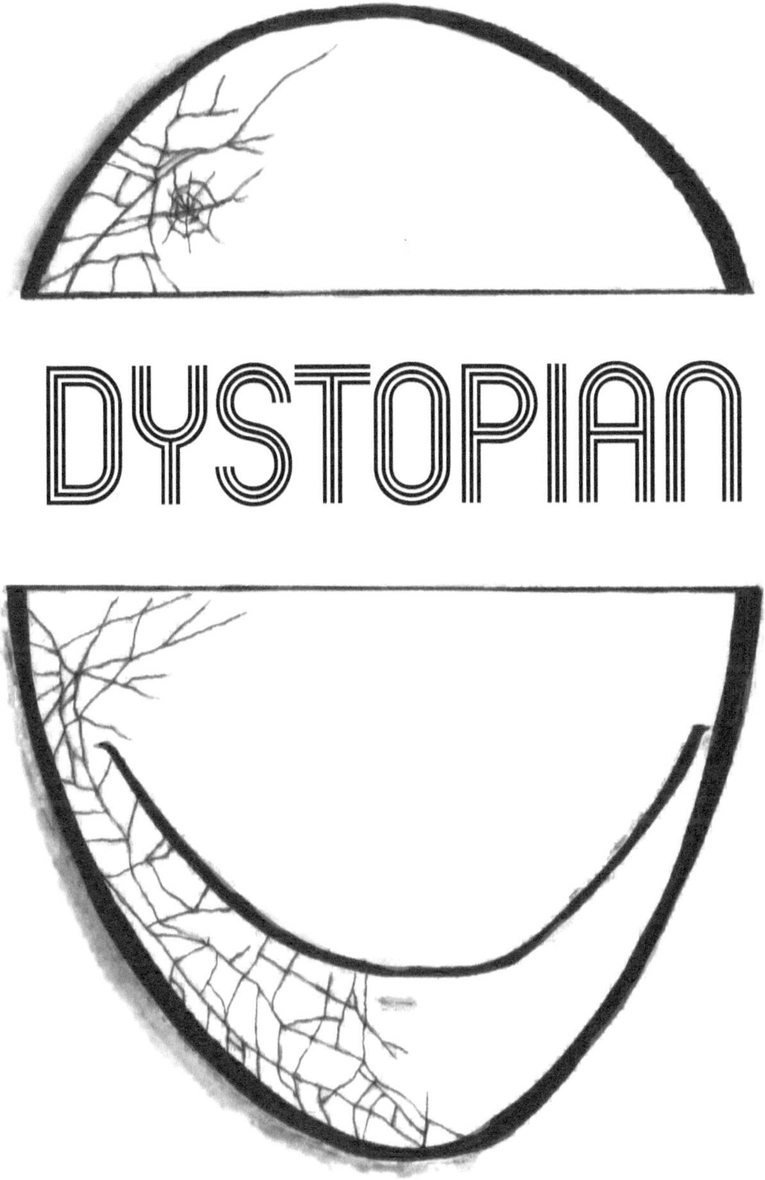

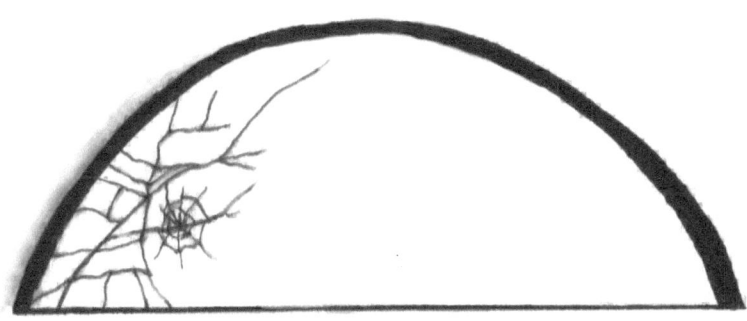

The Gemini Project

The tapping of her shoes echoed throughout the empty hallway as she walked to her office. It was six o'clock in the morning and the rest of her team wouldn't be in for hours, but today was a very important day and she had a lot of work to do.

Dr. Emilia Sanders was an employee of Zodiac Industries. At 32 she was the youngest project manager in the company, but she had always been an over-achiever. In her youth she was a science prodigy, and in university she completed degrees in Biology, Chemistry, Physics, and Engineering – all before she was 24 years old. After her studies she went to work for the government in their Environmental Technology Department, but after five years the entire department was defunded and disassembled.

After that, she discovered Zodiac Industries and learned how they were one of the few environmental research groups left in the world. Other companies, including the government, had given up on environmentalism altogether. Overpopulation had stretched the earth's natural resources to the breaking point, and space became a luxury that very few people could afford. Cities were overcrowded, filled with tall skyscrapers and small rooms. There weren't enough jobs to accommodate all of the population, which increased the percentage of unemployed and homeless.

The Earth was dying and humans were too miserable to notice.

Dr. Sanders used to live in the city, in a 10x15 foot bachelor apartment on the 34th floor of Complex J-216. Because of her government work she had been able to afford a larger room than most. When she was hired by Zodiac she gave up her apartment and moved into the compound. Not only did she have a much larger living space, but she was closer to her work.

After making herself a cup of synthetic coffee, she went to her office to go over all of the data for the current subjects. Reading through the reports helped calm the butterflies in her stomach, assuring her that they were ready for today's demonstration. By the time her team came in at eight o'clock, she was on her second cup.

Breakfast for the subjects was at 8:30am, so she waited until 8:45am before leaving her office. The first room was located on Level 2, Wing A. Dr. Sanders stopped at the prep-room across the hall to put on a containment suit before going inside.

In the room was a ten year old girl with light green eyes, straight brown hair, and a round face. She was wearing a light blue dress with black patent shoes, and had a white medical band around her wrist. The chair she was sitting on was too tall, and she swung her feet in the air as she ate her Synth-Os. The Vid-Screen in front of her played a bright cartoon, which was holding the child's attention.

"Good morning Abby," Dr. Sanders said as she entered the room, being careful not to get too close. "How are you today?"

"Fine," the girl said with her mouth full, not taking her eyes off the screen. "My arm itches."

"Is that because of the medication?"

The girl nodded. She finished the last spoonful and shoved the bowl aside.

"I have good news," Dr. Sanders said cheerfully. "Those were your last shots."

Abby turned away from the Vid-Screen so quickly that she almost fell off her chair. "It was?!"

"We just have to wait a couple of hours for the medication to start working, but after that you'll have a clean bill of health."

"What about -"

She nodded and Abby squealed in delight.

Dr. Sanders left after that, going back to the prep-room. She removed the containment suit and placed it in a sterilization container, being sure to carefully wash her hands afterward. Then she smoothed the wrinkles in her clothing, and headed towards Wing B. There she went into another prep-room, and put on another suit.

Inside the second room was a girl who looked exactly like Abby, except the medical band around her wrist was black instead of white.

"Good morning Ally," Dr. Sanders greeted cheerfully. "How are you today?"

The girl looked up at the doctor. Her Synth-Os were untouched, and she was barely looking at her Vid-Screen.

"Fine," the girl replied in an flat tone.

"Are you not hungry?"

"Not really."

"Is that because of the medication?"

The girl shrugged. Her right hand subconsciously went to her left arm, where the shots had been administered.

Dr. Sanders felt herself start to frown, so she quickly

plastered a smile on her face. "Ally, I know that the past 2 weeks have been difficult, but I have good news. Those were your last shots. You're all better now."

The girl's face broke out into a smile before quickly becoming serious again. "What about Abby?"

"Abby's fine too. We just need a few hours for the last of the medication to work and then you'll be together. All I ask is that you try to eat your cereal so you have enough energy for today."

The girl obediently began to eat her breakfast. Dr. Sanders left the room, removing the suit and washing her hands again before going back to her office.

She selected the Vox program on her computer and began to dictate.

"Doctor Emilia Sanders, Manager of the Gemini Project for Zodiac Industries. The date is April 30, 2217. The time is 9:40am. Today the final shots were administered and the subjects are ready. Subject Castor-14 reported of itching around the shot area, but no other side-effects. Subject Pollux-14 appears to have itching as well. She also has a loss of appetite, which could be the result of isolation instead of the medication. The demonstration has been scheduled for 11:15am."

When she finished she encoded the report and saved it in a folder on the main network. After that, she headed to the observation room to make sure that everything was ready. The spectators would be arriving at 11am, so there would not be much time between their arrival and the demonstration. Once everything was satisfactory, she headed back to her office to wait.

Shortly after 11am Doctor Ty Leonard, one of the co-founders of Zodiac Industries, lead a group of 20 people into the laboratory. The group consisted of people aged

20-30, of varying races and body types, but there was one distinction – they were all twins and all identical. They had been put through extensive screenings and tests before they had been authorized to view this demonstration. Zodiac's work was too important to risk letting the wrong person inside.

"This is Dr. Emilia Sanders," Dr. Leonard said, introducing her to the group. "She is the head of the Gemini Project and one of our brightest minds."

"Thank you for coming today," Dr. Sanders said. She could feel her heart rate speeding up, so she quickly reminded herself that she had no need to worry.

"You have all been briefed on the Gemini Project," she continued, "so I will not waste time talking about what you are here to see. Instead I will tell you why this project is so important. To put it simply, the Earth is dying. A regression in reproductive rights, coupled with the Birth-Control Sabotage of 2054, resulted in a major population burst – one which the Earth could barely support. Our resources have all but dried up and our days on this planet are numbered. While other companies have given up, Zodiac Industries is committed to finding a solution. This is where the Gemini Project comes in. This is where *you* come in."

She led the group to the observation room on the ground floor. For safety reasons, the demonstration would occur in an abandoned warehouse 10 miles away, but they would be able to watch everything from here. The warehouse had been made up to look like a park, with fake grass on the ground, and benches and picnic tables placed throughout the room. They had tried to make the fluorescent lights look liked sunlight, but there was still something vaguely unnatural about it.

The room was the equivalent of ten square city blocks. A variety of people were scattered throughout the room, reading, talking, or just enjoying the day. Dr. Sanders spoke into a microphone, giving the go-ahead.

A door opened on either end of the warehouse. Abby entered through the right door, and Ally through the left. Their faces were full of concentration as they walked a straight line towards the centre of the room, obediently following the instructions that had been given to them. Large smiles broke out on their faces as they saw each other, but they maintained their steady pace. Once they had stepped into the circle painted in the centre of the room, they reached out and shook hands for a few seconds before breaking formalities and hugging each other.

Clasping hands, they began to walk away, but they had only taken a few steps before Abby's legs gave out and she fell to the floor. Ally turned to help her, but her legs also buckled beneath her. The girls stared at each other, faces filled with confusion, before their eyes rolled back and they collapsed.

Slowly the inhabitants of the room began to realize that something was not right. Some moved closer to the girls, to see if they could help, while others moved further away. A minute later some of the people began to cough – small and quiet at first, but eventually turning into violent hacking coughs that shook their entire bodies. The cough spread throughout the warehouse, affecting some but not others. Those who were not coughing were looking around the scene, wondering what was happening and if it was going to happen to them next.

Dr. Sanders turned away from the screen.

"The subjects were instructed to walk to the centre of the room and shake hands," she explained to the group.

"The longer you maintain skin to skin contact the more potent the reaction will be. There is a radius of about 5 city blocks from Ground Zero – 4.7 blocks to be more precise. The virus is airborne and will infect anyone inside the radius within a minute. There is a short period of time where the infected can spread the virus to others within a two foot radius."

"Why were some people unaffected?" one of the visitors asked.

"They were injected with an antidote. The antidote will protect a person no matter how close to Ground Zero they are. As always, there is a slight probability that the antidote will not work, but the likelihood is very small – approximately 0.14%."

"Couldn't the subjects be given the antidote?" another visitor asked.

Dr. Sanders shook her head. "We tried to protect the subjects, but the virus was severely weakened, barely able to reach half of a city block. In order to maximize the effect, death is an unfortunate necessity. This is why we work with identical twins, so that we can achieve the best reaction. As you know, you have all been subjected to tests to see if your DNA is within the necessary threshold."

"Where do these people come from?" Someone asked, gesturing to the screens.

"Our hosts, designated Castor and Pollux, were adopted by the company after their parents were killed in a car accident. They were found to have a very rare medical condition and would not have survived much longer. The other people in the room were volunteers for a medical study – the unemployed or homeless looking for a way to make some money. They all knew the risk involved."

"Just another way that we are combating overpopulation," Dr. Leonard added.

The crowd nodded, and Dr. Sanders continued.

"The virus will take hold within ten minutes and will kill within three days. For the hosts death usually occurs within one minute, the average being forty-five seconds and the longest remaining alive for three minutes and fourteen seconds. Maintained contact not only helps the virus' strength but also ensures a quicker death. You should all remember that."

"We will be stationing each pair in a different city around the world," Dr. Leonard informed them. "If you stay within your designated area you should not come across each other until the designated meeting time. Due to the delicate nature of this project you will not be assigned to a city until just before the active date."

"It will take 2 weeks for preparation," Dr. Sanders added, "during which you will all be isolated. Once the preparations are completed you will be able to interact with regular people and live a normal life. The virus will remain dormant until you have skin to skin contact with your twin."

"Thank you Dr. Sanders," Dr. Leonard said. "Now, if the group will follow me back to my office, we have a few more details to go over."

He led the group away from the observation room, but a set of female twins hung back.

"You worked on the Land-Jumper Project for the government, didn't you?" the girl on the left asked Dr. Sanders.

"Yes, I did." She raised an eyebrow, confused about how they would know that. The Land-Jumper was supposed to be a new way of air-travel, using condensed propulsion to shoot a travel pod up into the air and glide towards its destination. The Land-Jumper would have used less fuel than Air-Jets and would not pollute the atmosphere. It was close to being finished when the government decided to pull the plug because the project was deemed unfeasible.

"Our father worked on the same project – Dr. Henry Steingraff."

"Oh, yes. How is he doing?"

"Good. He's working on the Mars Development Project now."

Dr. Sanders nodded. "Most of the Land-Jumper team went over to that project."

"Everyone except for you," the twin on the right said.

"I considered it, but I decided that I'd rather try to save the planet we have now before dumping our problems onto another planet."

"Zodiac Industries is doing great work. If our dad knew what they were really up to he might not agree with their methods, but we do."

"I'm glad," Dr. Sanders smiled. "It's people like you who are going to help us bring this planet back to life. Your sacrifice is going to cause a lot of good."

The young women said a quick goodbye and hurried to catch up with the group. Dr. Sanders watched them go before heading back to her lab. Her team was eagerly waiting to hear the results.

"The demonstration went very well," she informed them. "We'll analyze the results once the clean-up team has finished with the warehouse. Another 2 or 3 demonstrations and we should have enough recruits to put the plan into motion. Now, how are Castor-15 and Pollux-15?"

"They're well," a member of her team replied. "Side-effects are within normal parameters. They'll be ready for their demonstration next week." He looked up from his notes. "I heard that the Taurus Project is ready to go at any time. They're just waiting on us."

"Of course they are," Dr. Sanders replied, unable to keep the annoyance out of her voice. "The Taurus Project simply has to blow up a number of tech buildings. Their work with explosives is child's play compared to what we're doing. Even the Virgo Project isn't as scientifically complicated as ours. They're simply tainting various water supplies with birth control, while we're working with genetic codes."

"Speaking of child's play, we have Castor-16 and Pollux-16 arriving tomorrow. Males, age 8 years old."

"Orphans again, I presume."

He referred to his notes again. "Parents and older sibling recently killed in a car crash. No remaining family."

Dr. Sanders nodded. "There really are a lot of car crashes these days..."

Authentic New Island Experience™

Looking for an exciting place to travel? Why not visit New Island Ltd.! Formerly known as Newfoundland, trust us when we say the only thing that's changed is the name! Experience our stunning vistas and breath-taking views, while enjoying the Authentic New Island Personalities™ that the island is known for. Wander through one of our many small towns and admire the natural scenery while getting to know the local characters. Or, if you're looking for a more modern experience, visit the bustling city of New St. John's where you can grab a pint with a pal and dine on the finest local delicacies!

Worried about your daily consumer allowance while on the island? Don't be! Purchase a Local Traveller's Pass to cover all your basic needs or get more bang for your buck with a High Roller's Pass. Or upgrade to an Unlimited Pass and consume as much as you desire! Whatever your needs are, we have a Pass for you!

See majestic ocean creatures on a whale watching boat ride or travel north on an iceberg tour! Hike the magnificent mountains of Gros Morne Park or discover the magic of Lanse Aux Meadows! Get 'Screeched In' and eat as much Jigg's Dinner as you can handle! New Island Ltd. has it all!

There was a brief moment of silence as the commercial ended, the jingling tune fading into nothingness as the logo for New Island Ltd. appeared on the screen. The logo remained for a few seconds before changing into an image of rolling waves beneath a cliff. The jingle started up again and the commercial repeated itself for the seventh time.

As much as Dana hated the commercial, she couldn't handle the silence of the apartment. She needed some kind of sound in the background, and this was the only channel that didn't cost any money to watch.

If Jocelyn had been here, she would have told Dana to turn the television off before that jingle drove her insane. She also would have told her to stop crying so much. All those tears would surely dehydrate her, and she'd run the risk of going over her daily water allowance.

But that was the problem. That was why Dana couldn't stop crying.

Jocelyn wasn't here.

©

"How ya' gettin' on?"

Dana snapped back into reality. The lush green forest she'd been dreaming of was replaced by the hard, plastic truth of the Valley Mall food court she was currently sitting in. Grass, leaves, and sunshine quickly transformed into Some Nice™ restaurants and Best Sort™ shops that populated malls all across the island.

Turning to her right, Dana looked up at the smiling brunette whose cheerful voice had shattered her daydream.

"Are you Jocelyn?" she asked.

The brunette nodded. "Sorry I'm late. There was a hell o'va line up at Timmy's. Should'a known better than th' think there wouldn't be a line up at th' mall." She took a sip from the cup in her hand and sat down across from Dana. "So, yer lookin' for a roomie?"

Nodding slowly, Dana wondered what she'd gotten herself in to. When they'd spoken over the phone to set up the meeting, Jocelyn hadn't sounded so... small town.

"And you're looking to move out of the boarding house?" Dana asked, trying to keep her voice pleasant.

Jocelyn smiled. "Yup. Gotta feel some freedom under me wings. Them women running th' boardin' houses got eyes like hawks. Can barely take a breath without one of 'em knowin'."

Dana tried to return the smile, but she knew it must look forced. "And the price of rent won't be a problem?"

She nodded again. "I gotta job at th' Some Nice™ Bakery on West Street, sos I can afford th' rent. I assumes all th' taxes are included? Water, electricity, police, fire, whatnot?"

"They are. We get a bit of a break, because there are two apartments in the house, so we share the city maintenance and local maintenance taxes with the other tenants. Also, the landlord's an old family friend who babysat me when I was younger, so he was able to give me the family rate instead of the unmarried woman's rate."

"Ah, that's why th' rent's so affordable," she smirked. "Heck, I'd let someone babysit me now if it'd get me a deal like tha' one."

Dana couldn't help laughing. It seemed that Jocelyn had a sense of humour, which was encouraging. "Would you like to see the apartment?" she asked. "It's only one block away."

Jocelyn's eyes widened. "You lives near th' mall? Whatta grand deal. I'd love ta see th' place."

Dana stood up and gestured for Jocelyn to follow her.

She barely said anything during the walk, as Jocelyn didn't stop talking about what it had been like to move from Rocky Harbour to Corner Brook. Every word was pleasant and absolutely dripping with her North-coast accent. Dana wondered if the accent would lessen after a few years of living here or if it'd stay that way forever. As much as she didn't want to give up her apartment and move into one of those boarding houses, she wasn't sure if she could handle listening to that every single day.

They quickly reached the apartment, which was on the second floor of a former two-story house. "So, what'd happened ta your old roomie?" Jocelyn asked as they made their way through the apartment. "Oh, sorry," she said, stopping in her tracks. She paused and took a moment to compose herself. "So, what happened to the person you were living with? Why did she move out?"

It took Dana a few seconds to comprehend what had just been said. The un-accented words sounded as if they should be coming from someone else's mouth, but there was nobody else around.

Jocelyn laughed. "Sorry about that. You know what it's like growing up in a Designated Small Town. All accent, all the time. It's a hard habit to shake."

"Wow." Dana was truly taken aback. "You sound so normal now. Not that – I mean – it's just that... Oh, god..." She put her head in her hands. She needed to stop talking.

"It's okay," Jocelyn said, her voice light and cheerful. "After eighteen years in a DST, it's hard not to put the accent on whenever I'm in public. I always get paranoid that tourists might be within earshot, and I've made it this many years without getting fined for 'ruining the illusion'." She dramatically rolled her eyes.

Dana laughed, feeling the tension melting away. "Sorry. I grew up in Corner Brook, so I've never had to deal with laws that strict. I can't imagine what it's like."

"Honestly, it's like anything else – you get used to it. But it's refreshing to live somewhere that you can relax. Performing 24/7 is *exhausting*." Jocelyn sat down on the couch. "But I was asking about your previous roommate. Do you mind talking about her?"

She shook her head. "Erin... Erin had been friends with me since junior high. When we moved in here, we knew that it was only a matter of time before her boyfriend proposed and she'd get married and they'd get a house to live in. Sure enough, a few months later, he did, and they started wedding planning. Then, a few weeks ago, about two months before the wedding, his relatives in Nova Scotia contacted him, saying that they were willing to sponsor his move off the island. The only problem was that they couldn't afford to sponsor two people. He didn't want this opportunity to pass him by, so he called off the wedding, did up the paperwork, and moved away. After that, Erin married the first decent guy she came across and moved out. They've got a house up on Glenhaven Boulevard."

Jocelyn let out a slow breath. "Wow. That sucks."

"Yeah. Makes me never want to get my hopes up. About anything."

"Well, if it helps my application, I don't plan on getting married any time soon." Jocelyn smiled.

Dana returned the smile. "It definitely tips the scales in your favour."

©

Jocelyn moved in a few days later and the two of them quickly grew close. At first Dana found the way that Jocelyn unconsciously slipped into her old accent a bit much, but she knew that it wasn't done on purpose. Jocelyn was a genuinely nice person, and Dana was glad to have met her – even with all of her Designated Small Town tendencies.

"You've got to play the game," Jocelyn said, tapping Dana playfully on the nose.

Dana frowned and waved Jocelyn's hand away. She'd come home from her date early, having decided that enough was enough two hours in. She'd been hoping her roommate would offer commiseration, but apparently that wasn't to be the case.

"I don't want to," Dana complained, walking over to the couch and falling onto it dramatically. "Dating is stupid."

"It won't kill you," Jocelyn replied, crossing her arms. "You know, you always have to make things more difficult than they actually are."

Dana frowned again. She wasn't the person who'd thought of mandatory dating for all citizens, or the person who'd included it in Govern-Corp's Tourism Laws, so how was she the difficult one? It wasn't her fault that the guy she'd gone out with tonight had been utterly wrong for her, so why should she be punished for not wanting to go out with him again?

Jocelyn sat down next to her. "The Rom-Cops will be easier on you if you look like you're making an effort. You don't have to get married, just date him for a few months before making up an excuse to dump him, and then move on to the next guy."

"But it's so stupid..."

"You know that if you don't go on a date at least once a week, you'll be fined. And you've already got two fines on your record. A few more of those and they'll get suspicious and investigate you, which wouldn't be good for either of us." Jocelyn gave her a knowing a look. "Do you want to end up in a detention centre for the rest of your life – or worse – all because you didn't want to go on a few stupid dates?"

Dana sighed. "I know, I know. I'm just tired of it all."

"Well, grab a cup of Some Nice™ coffee, get your second wind, and suck it up."

She gave Jocelyn an unimpressed look. "I cannot believe you just said that."

Jocelyn smirked. "You can take the girl out of the DST, but you can't take the DST out of the girl."

It would be wise to take Jocelyn's advice, and Dana knew it. Jocelyn knew how to look like she was following the government's rules while secretly maintaining her own agenda. Her pleasant attitude and friendliness with tourists had been noted by Govern-Corp, and whenever she'd 'accidentally' stepped out of line, they'd been much more lenient with her than they would with any other citizen.

Citizens living in DSTs were paid to act like charming locals for the tourists, and with the high cost of living on New Island Ltd., not many of them could afford not to. Living in a DST meant being constantly aware of the Quality Control Agents who patrolled the whole island, writing up anyone who was caught out of character or causing trouble for Govern-Corp.

It sounded like the worst kind of life to Dana, who'd surely be in a detention centre by now if she'd been unlucky enough to be born in a DST. Corner Brook was the perfect size for her – too big to be a quaint small town, but too small to be as bustling as the capital city. They still had to be friendly and nice to all the tourists, but not at the same level as those in DSTs.

"But he talked through the entire movie," Dana groaned, unable to let the subject drop. "It's been so long since I've been to one, and he had to ruin it with his incessant chatter."

Jocelyn laughed. "You could have simply avoided the movies next time."

"Ugh. When you say things like that it sounds so... rational." She sat up and put her head on Dana's shoulder. "I just wish that I could date who I wanted."

"*The mandate of Govern-Corp is to promote the prosperity of New Island Ltd. and all its citizens through a rich tourism trade, which includes creating a safe, non-political environment where tourists from all over the world will not feel uncomfortable.*" When Jocelyn finished quoting policy, she kissed Dana on top of her head. "At least they can't govern us inside our home."

A smile appeared on Dana's face. "Yeah. At least we have that."

Outside these walls they could never be anything more than friends, but in here nobody could tell them that what they felt was wrong.

"Have you ever wondered what it would be like to live normally?" Jocelyn asked softly. "Before Govern-Corp purchased this island and the Tourism Laws were passed?"

"All the time," Dana replied honestly.

"What if it were possible? What if we could?"

She straightened up. "What are you talking about?"

Jocelyn leaned in close and her voice went low. "Vineland."

Dana was confused. "You mean, what the Vikings called this island back in 1000 AD? Are you talking about the Viking settlement at Lanse Aux Meadows? That's even more tourist-themed than Rocky Harbour."

"No," Jocelyn shook her head. "The new Vineland. Surely you've heard the rumours. No Tourism Laws, no taxes or fines... It's the promised land."

It sounded vaguely familiar to Dana, but in a fairy-tale kind of way. Vineland was a fantasy for adults, a long-abandoned settlement that had been reclaimed by people sick of living under Govern-Corp's rules. It was supposed to be like the good old days, before Canada sold the island and all its resources to Govern-Corp for a tidy sum, and it was most likely a complete and total fiction.

Anyone who talked openly about going there was never heard from again. Some dreamed that those people had actually made it to Vineland, but Dana wasn't so optimistic. They had most likely 'disappeared', like the majority of the island's unhappy locals. Troublemakers didn't last long on New Island Ltd.

"Vineland's a fantasy," she replied. "It doesn't exist."

Jocelyn gave her shoulder a squeeze. "Ah, there's that pessimism I love so much."

"If it existed, I'm sure Govern-Corp would quash it. They'd destroy something like that twenty times over."

"But," Jocelyn was getting excited again. "It would actually be in their best interest to have a place like that. Somewhere for the rabble to go, to stay away from tourists, and stop us from being so contrary in front of them. The existence of Vineland benefits everyone."

Her enthusiasm was infectious, but Dana couldn't stop worrying.

"Still..." Dana said. "It's illegal to move without alerting Populace Control. What if they find out what we're doing and have us arrested or put in some dark hole for the rest of our lives?" There were more than enough stories about locals who didn't obey the Tourism Laws and had to be rehabilitated, or sent to detention centres, or forced to work in mines, never seeing the sunlight ever again. Did she really want to risk her comfortable life for something that didn't exist?

"And what if we're very, very careful and we don't get caught?" Jocelyn's eyes pleaded with her. "Haven't you ever wanted more than this? Haven't you ever wanted to live on your own terms?"

Dana frowned. Honestly, she'd never thought of a life other than this one. Sometimes she'd dream about what it would be like to live somewhere not ruled by Govern-Corp, but it was a pipe dream – something that would never happen. She didn't have rich relatives who could sponsor a move off the island, and she'd never be able to save up enough, so why bother dreaming about it?

Although she still had her doubts, Dana had a feeling that Jocelyn would try to find Vineland no matter what. If she agreed to this crazy plan, then at least she could try to keep Jocelyn safe.

Maybe they'd discover that Vineland actually did exist. And if it didn't, at least they'd still be together.

Dana sighed. "You have to promise me that you'll be careful? That we'll be careful?"

Jocelyn's eyes lit up. "I promise."

©

It was all going according to plan, until Jocelyn fell ill. One day she was fine, and the next she was in the hospital with Viral Strain 14. Dana had no idea how it happened or how she'd avoided getting the virus as well, but even though the doctors explained that VS-14 only affected a small percentage of the population, Dana was too paranoid to be comforted.

Had Govern-Corp somehow realized what they were planning? Had Jocelyn said something to the wrong person? Asked the wrong question? Drawn attention to herself?

They'd spent the past five months slowly gathering supplies and information, even going on camping trips in Gros Morne to account for the purchase of certain items, like lamps and bedrolls and backpacks. Dana didn't think that they'd done anything out of the ordinary, but how could she really know?

It was possible that she was overthinking this. Jocelyn's illness could very well have been natural. It might have happened no matter what.

Then again, it wasn't unusual for Govern-Corp's enemies to come down with life-threatening illnesses. There were twenty-three Viral Strains on record, and almost every person who'd passed away from them had been known trouble-makers. Had Jocelyn's name found her way on one of Govern-Corp lists? Was Dana's name also on a list?

Jocelyn had tried to calm Dana's fears, but both of them knew that Jocelyn would never leave the hospital. As the hours passed, she grew sicker and sicker, and nothing the doctors did seemed to make any difference.

Throughout Jocelyn's quick and deadly illness, Dana had to pretend to be a friend and was only allowed to visit during general visiting hours. Whenever she complained about how unfair it was, which was a lot, Jocelyn would smile and tell her to "play the game." More than ever Dana wished that there wasn't a game to play.

She hadn't been there at the end, which was one of

her biggest regrets. She should have tried harder or made up some kind of lie. Even though she knew that Jocelyn wouldn't want her to take unnecessary risks, Dana wished that she'd been there.

She could still hear Jocelyn's last words to her, echoing inside her head. "Be happy," Jocelyn had said, but that seemed impossible now. Dana had no idea what she was going to do without her. All she could manage was to sit in the apartment they'd once shared and cry.

Her gaze fell on the two backpacks in the corner of the room. If things had gone as planned, Jocelyn and she would leave for Vineland next week, but now that would never happen.

It would make sense for Dana to stay here and continue her life, but in the moment that Jocelyn took her last breath, everything had changed. Dana didn't want this. She didn't want to live in a world where she couldn't hold her partner's hand in public, where she had to hide her feelings and pretend to be 'normal', all because some corporation was afraid that her actions might cause controversy. She wanted to live somewhere where she could stay by her partner's hospital bed day and night, where she didn't have to be so afraid.

Wiping the tears from her eyes, she stood up and walked over to the backpacks.

©

This was the part Dana was most afraid of. This was where everything could go terribly wrong.

There weren't many other cars on the highway this late at night. With the high cost of gas, vehicle registration, and licence fees, most people couldn't afford to drive. The only reason Dana had a car was because her parents had gifted it to her before retiring in Twillingate. She'd never bothered to drive it before meeting Jocelyn, but it had become integral to their plan.

Outside Corner Brook, she stopped at a gas station along the highway to purchase a snack and fill up the tank before continuing on. She felt strangely calm, but as she took the turn towards the Port au Port Peninsula, her stomach filled with a horde of nervous butterflies.

Twenty minutes after the turn off, she reached the spot. Taking in a deep breath, Dana pressed down on the gas pedal. She turned the wheel sharply to her right before slamming on the brakes and swinging the wheel to the left. The car sped across the highway and drove off the road, heading for the trees. As the car bounced and jumped over the uneven terrain, Dana was glad she'd tightened her seatbelt, although that didn't stop her head from taking a nasty bump against the door. Luckily the airbags deployed as soon as the front of the car crashed into a tree.

When it was all over, Dana sat in the car for a few minutes, trying to pull herself together. Her body felt sore and shaken, but she could still wiggle her fingers and toes, and her arms and legs worked. Her head hurt, but at least it was still on her neck.

Unbuckling her seatbelt, she opened the door and spilled out on to the ground. There were so many aches and pains that she was afraid to stop and list them, lest she be here for days. Pulling herself up onto her feet, she leaned against the car for a few seconds before moving on with the plan.

Opening the back door, she pulled off the blanket covering the two backpacks and removed everything from the car. If the information Jocelyn had gathered was correct, then she should have more than enough provisions to make the journey. She rolled up the blanket, shoved it into one of the backpacks, and shut the door.

When someone inevitably found her car, hopefully they'd assume that she'd gone off the road accidentally, wandered into the woods while disoriented, and died of exposure. It was common for people to crash while trying to avoid hitting moose or other animals. Besides, who would fill up a gas tank before purposefully crashing their car – especially at these prices?

After checking that there was nobody else on the highway, she turned on her flashlight and looked towards the woods. Vineland was supposed to be hidden in there, somewhere. Hopefully it was. Hopefully she wouldn't die out here alone.

There was still time for her to give up, to stop this crazy plan, ditch the backpacks, and stay with the car. Someone would find her and bring her back to Corner Brook. She could go back to the life she knew and learn to cope, learn to adjust. Learn to settle for less.

But Dana didn't want that. She didn't want to bow down to a corporation that cared more about lining its pockets than the people who worked for it. She wanted revenge, she wanted happiness, she wanted freedom...

She wanted more.

Shouldering the backpacks, she walked towards the woods.

Game Plan

As John half-listened to his co-workers talk about how their lives were so much better under The Emperor's rule, he imagined how wonderful it would be once the Resistance swarmed the palace and killed them all. He had spent the past four months working in the palace, making friends with the other employees, and proving himself to be trustworthy, but secretly he had been placed there by the Resistance. It had been exhausting to keep up the charade for so long, but he was fuelled by his conviction that the world would be a better place once The Emperor was dead.

Although he was too young to recall how life had been before The Emperor took control of the government, the elders remembered. They told stories of democracy and freedom, where people were allowed to choose where they worked, where they lived, and who they loved – when citizens could go for a walk without worrying that they might be arrested for no discernable reason. Nowadays everyone's life was controlled by The Emperor, except for those within the Resistance, who hid from the prying eyes of the militia and spent most of their time plotting to bring down The Emperor and end his tyrannical rule.

The elders had been hesitant about John's long-term plan, not wanting to wait so many months for action, but he had convinced them that it would be necessary. The more time he had, the more trusted he'd be, and the easier it would be to infiltrate the palace's security.

And, good as his word, he had done just that. He'd memorized layouts, cultivated relationships, and learned what time would be the best for an attack. Tonight he would put the final part of his plan into motion. Tonight he would taste success.

Although he had a job on the palace cleaning staff, he'd made friends with many of the security workers, and a few weeks ago they started inviting him to their after-work gatherings. When their shift was over, they'd go to an unoccupied room in the basement to drink, laugh, and talk about how great life was for them. They believed wholeheartedly in The Emperor and his master plan and enjoyed the power they received as part of the palace security staff. Although it disgusted John beyond belief, he played along, smiling and laughing, and pretending to be one of them.

Tonight, however, he was done with playing. He waited an appropriate length of time before snapping his fingers and declaring that he'd left his coat in the employee room. He informed the group that he'd be back in a few minutes and not to drink everything without him. They laughed and went back to their discussion before he'd left the room.

That was the easy part. The employee room was on the first floor, but he had to make it to the third floor without being spotted. Earlier he'd lifted Everett's key-card from his pocket, since Everett had worked here the longest and had the highest security clearance. Providence seemed to be on John's side as Everett's key-card had no trouble unlocking the door to the third floor. The hall was empty as he made his way towards the electrical room, and one quick wave of the key-card triggered the sensor and unlocked the door.

Most of the palace's electricity was wired through this room, including the security fences. John slipped inside and quickly got to work, first turning the electricity off before setting about destroying the wires and fuses. The Resistance fighters were hidden outside, waiting for the hum of the electric fences to go quiet so that they could charge into the palace and kill their oppressors.

He wished that there were windows in the room, so that he could see the fighters charging. The security teams had grown soft, confident in their secure surroundings, so they would be easily overpowered. Without electricity, the palace wouldn't be able to go into panic mode and every room, and every person, would be accessible.

As much as John wanted to be out there, fighting amongst his people, he knew that he had to make sure the electricity stayed down. Maybe someone would come in here and find him, and maybe he would be killed, but if the Resistance succeeded, his death would be worth it.

***

"Simulation over. Kill count is one hundred and fourteen, including The Emperor. The palace has fallen."

Kline removed the VR helmet and let out a substantial sigh. Even with an accelerated time rate, spending four months in virtual reality was a long time.

"Great job, sir," a young man said as he walked over to take the helmet. "We've had fourteen others try the simulation and none of them came close to succeeding."

"Of course not," Kline said, fighting the urge to roll his eyes. If you wanted something done right...

There were four computers along the far wall and in

front of each was an employee quickly extrapolating the data from the simulation.

"This will be very helpful, sir," the young man continued, putting the helmet back on the equipment table. "We thought that we had covered all the bases, but you've done it again. We had no idea that someone would risk going undercover for so long."

"You'd be surprised what some people are capable of when they truly believe in something."

The young man smiled. "I'd be surprised if there was another person on this planet who was as capable as you. You have an incomparable mind and an awe-inspiring ability to solve any problem."

Kline couldn't help smiling at the compliment. "That's what makes me The Emperor." He straightened his suit and walked towards the door. "I know that you still have data to extrapolate, but I'd suggest that we immediately obtain backup generators for the security fences and palace grid."

The man nodded enthusiastically. "Long live the Emperor."

Kline held back a satisfied laugh. Yes, long live me.

HUMOUR

What's in a Name?

Their pursuit was relentless, and although William ran as if his life depended on it, it wasn't enough. Exhaustion overtook him and he stumbled, falling to the ground. Mud coated his hands and knees, and though his mind yelled at his body to get up and keep going, his muscles were too tired to obey.

The three figures quickly caught up to him. They wore long, black, hooded robes and their faces were hidden in shadow. He had no idea what they looked like, but he knew their voices – deep and low, each word reverberating through every part of his body. They weren't human. They terrified him.

"You have made us work hard," one of the figures said.

"We do not like that," another finished.

Thoughts of escaping from their grasp were pointless. They had hounded him for hours, finding him no matter where he'd hidden, hunting him like a mouse in a maze. William didn't know what they wanted, but he was too exhausted to fight anymore.

"You have broken our laws," one of them said.

"And for that you must be punished."

William shook his head. "What laws have I broken? What am I accused of?" He tried to think of something he might have done in the past few days or weeks or even months that would be worth such a terrifying experience, but nothing came to mind. Maybe, if he could find out what he was accused of, he could talk his way out of this.

"You know what you did."

He shook his head again. "I don't know. Honest."

"Ignorance is no excuse."

"The laws of the Ilvid are absolute."

"I know nothing of the Ilvid," William continued, "or your laws!"

"Lies will get you nowhere."

"But I'm not lying! What did I do? Maybe it was an honest mistake."

"You know well what you did."

"You transposed in full view of mortals."

"A transgression punishable by death."

Now he was even more confused. "What the heck is transposing?"

"You may feign ignorance if you wish, but it will not change what you have done."

"You have broken the laws."

"And for that you will die, William Eric DeGrace."

His eyes opened wide. "Hold on a second! My middle name's not Eric, it's Eugene. I'm William Eugene De-Grace."

The hooded figures paused and turned to each other.

"William Eugene DeGrace?"

"Is it possible that we are mistaken?"

One of the hooded figures moved closer to William, taking in his features. "He does look very much like the William we are after."

Another stepped up. "However, there are differences."

"Then it would appear that we have the wrong man."

The hooded figures huddled together and whispered in low voices. Finally they broke apart.

"Sorry about that, mate," one of them said in an Australian accent. "Bit of an admin mix-up, eh?"

"You're free to leave," said another with a soft Southern accent.

"Yes, and we're ever so sorry about the whole mistaken identity thing," a British accent added.

William cautiously stood up, a mixture of relief and confusion swirling inside him. "Uh, well, thanks, I guess." He took a half-step back, expecting them to stop him, but they didn't move. The Australian one actually raised a hand and waved goodbye. William quickly raced away.

The Battle of San Remo

The vacation was off to a terrible start.

"Come out and face me like a proper Roman solider!" the voice on the other side of the door shouted.

I put my head in my hands and gave an exhausted sigh. Craig had been standing outside my hotel room, yelling challenges at me for the past twenty minutes. I'd thought that after a while he'd calm down, realize he was being an idiot and stop all this, but so far he showed no signs of stopping.

"I demand satisfaction!" he bellowed.

It started at the Colosseum, on our very first day in Rome. After taking a tour of the famous historical site, we saw a sign for Gladiator Classes and thought it would be fun to sign up. At first it was harmless, dressing in cheap plastic helmets, learning how to swing a practice sword and defend ourselves with a shield, but then we were pitted against each other. Craig and I faced off, and when I emerged as the obvious victor, Craig did not handle it well and instantly demanded a re-match. Thankfully, our class was almost over. We either had to pay for another session or leave, and since I didn't want to pay again I decided to get the heck out of there.

Craig, who was unable to take a hint, followed me back to our hotel, demanding another fight—much to the confusion of the many pedestrians we passed.

Once I arrived back at the Hotel San Remo, where we were staying, I went straight to my room and shut the door in Craig's face. I'd planned on waiting out his anger, but that was proving to be a fool's errand.

"I'm never going to fight you, Craig!" I yelled through the door. "So give up!"

"Never!" he shot back. "Alea iacta est!"

I sighed again and leaned against the door. A few seconds later I heard the sound of furniture being moved around. Looking through the peephole I watched Craig drag the chairs and tables that had been decorating the hallway, pushing them against my door. It was useless, because the door opened inward, but it would make my way out slightly more difficult.

"What are you doing?" I asked.

"I'm walling you in, Vercingetorix!"

"Who...? What did you just call me?"

"Give in now! I am the great strategist Julius Caesar and you are the Gaul scum who will starve in your walled city of Alesia! Soon hunger will get the best of you, you'll come out from behind this door, and I'll have my revenge!"

I wondered if maybe I should go out there and give Craig what he wanted before he destroyed the hotel, but I really didn't want to fight him. I was pretty sure I'd defeat him in any battle he wanted, which would only make him more determined. It would be useless trying to throw the fight—Craig was the kind of guy who, if he was winning, would trip on the carpet and knock himself out on the nearest wall.

"If you don't give this up, I'm going to call hotel security on you!" I yelled.

"Let them come! I'll be ready!" He gave a gleefully evil

laugh that would've made a madman smile with pride.

It was official—Craig had finally gone off the deep end.

I wondered why I hadn't bothered calling security before now. For that matter, why hadn't anyone else? Were the other guests on this floor out sightseeing and missing all the theatrics? As I walked over to the room phone, the sound of more furniture being moved distracted me. What the hell was Craig doing?

Through the peephole I could see that he had arraigned the furniture so that it not only blocked my door, but also blocked the path to the elevator. Sitting in between these two barricades, in the newly created no-mans-land, was Craig.

"What are you doing?" I asked.

"I'm walling myself in, just like Julius Caesar did. Go ahead, call security. They'll never make it through! Veni vidi vici!"

Shaking my head, I sat down on the bed and took out my cell phone. Connecting to the hotel's wi-fi, I tried to figure out what the hell he was talking about, as he continued to shout challenges through the door. Finally I found information about the Battle of Alesia in 52 BC, which was surprisingly similar to my current situation. I was doomed. Leave it to Craig to go insane and try to re-create a famous Roman battle while in Rome. Most people wanted to wear togas or drive Vespas, but he had to take tourist-hood to a whole new level.

If only there was some way that I could use history against him... My eyes fell on the wall calendar across the room and inspiration struck. Maybe the way out was easier than I thought.

One phone call and a very strange request later, I went

back to the door to talk to Craig.

"Give up! You're not going to win this battle. You're not Caesar."

"How dare you think such a thing!? Come and out say that to my face!"

I shook my head. "Fine, if you want to be Caesar, go for it. But you should remember that although the Battle of Alesia ended well for him, there was one particular day that did not."

The hallway went quiet.

"Do you remember what month it is, Craig?"

"Yeah... But it's the twenty-first," he replied, his voice shaking. "The Ides of March have passed."

"Then it seems that Caesar is long overdue for his *stabbing*!"

I heard a door open and when I looked through the peephole I saw a staff member of the Hotel San Remo emerge from the stairwell, standing tall and broad in his bright red vest and crisp white shirt. Craig might have been smart enough to put a barricade between him and the elevator, but he'd forgotten about the stairs.

"Hey Craig," I yelled out. "Want to know the concierge's name? I'll give you a hint. It starts with a 'B' and rhymes with 'suitest'."

Craig babbled unintelligibly.

"If you promise to never again ask me to fight you, I'll make him go away. But if you insist—"

"I'm done! No more fighting!"

Laughter rose up inside of me, but I held it back. Craig sounded legitimately terrified.

"Okay then." I opened up the door and looked out over the furniture, to where Craig was cowering behind a small table. I turned to the concierge, whose name was actually Leon. "Thank you, Sir."

He bowed his head. "I expect that this furniture will be returned to its proper place within the hour?"

I nodded at him and he turned around, disappearing into the stairwell.

When I looked back at Craig I could see that all the fight had gone out of him.

"Craig..." I began.

He looked up at me, ashamed.

"I'm never travelling anywhere with you. Ever. Again."

He nodded. "Yeah, I deserve that."

All Trades

Madeline wasn't sure what she'd expected The Jacks to look like, but it definitely wasn't like *this*. First off, despite calling themselves 'Jacks' they both appeared to be young women instead of the burly men she'd been expecting, and secondly, they looked nothing like a team.

The taller of the 2 had short red hair that was neatly gelled back. She was dressed in a bright green top, bright blue pants, and a white blazer. Her posture was picture-perfect as she sat in her chair, an open notebook and a large mug of tea on the table in front of her. She had broad shoulders and almost eclipsed the petite woman sitting next to her – who was slouched so far down in her chair that she might as well be sitting on the floor. The smaller woman was wearing all black and had her arms crossed over her chest. Her long black hair hung in front of her face, making it impossible to see her expression, but if Madeline had to make an educated guess she'd say that the second woman either scowling or asleep.

Perhaps she had the wrong date or maybe she was at the wrong tea house, but a quick look at her notebook, where she'd meticulously written down all the details, confirmed that this was the correct time and place. As she cautiously made her way to the table at the back of the tea house Madeline wondered what the chances were that The Jacks had been unable to make the meeting and two random strangers had wandered in and happened to sit at this particular table.

The red-head looked up from her notebook as she approached.

"Madeline?"

She nodded. So much for that thought. Hopefully these two were as good as their reputation.

"Would you like a drink? I can signal the waitress for you."

"Um, sure," Madeline replied, taking a seat across from the red-head.

The waitress came over right away and Madeline ordered a small cup of green tea. She'd never been a fan of tea but everyone drank green tea these days. It was supposed to be good for you or something.

Once the waitress was gone the red-head extended her right hand.

"We're The Jacks, but you can call me Xavier. And this is Burn," she said, gesturing to her partner.

"Really?" Madeline couldn't help laughing. "Your name is Burn?"

"Yes." The reply was flat and unamused.

She knew she should let it go, but couldn't. Xavier was a strange enough name for a woman but Burn? It was a verb, not a name. "Why would your parents call you *Burn*?"

The woman leaned forward, and as she did her hair parted, showing a serious face with dark grey eyes. "I wasn't always called Burn," she began in a low voice. "When I was a child I was fascinated with fire. I would let the candles on my birthday cakes burn out rather than extinguish them. When I was six I set fire to some pillows in the backyard. A week later I set fire to our shed, and three days later I set fire to a neighbours' house. After that my parents legally changed my name to Burn as a warning to all who met me."

Madeline was aghast. "Really?!"

She sighed and leaned back in her chair. "Of course not, you idiot. I'm named after an actor."

Madeline didn't know how to respond to that. Luckily the waitress returned with her tea, so she held the mug with both hands and took a sip, all the while wishing that she could disappear. This was definitely not the meeting she'd been expecting.

"Don't mind her," Xavier said with a large smile, "she's having an off day. Month, actually. We can talk about the reason for this meeting if you're ready to get down to business."

"Oh, yes." Madeline put down her mug and composed herself. "Well, I need some help and I heard that you two pretty much do anything for a price."

"Anything within reason. It may not look like it, but we have standards," Xavier said brightly.

Madeline nodded. Xavier probably had standards, but she wasn't so sure about the other one.

"So, back to your problem…"

"I need you to break into a building and get a file off one of the computers."

"That's it?" Xavier replied, confused. Madeline's frantic phone call the day before had led her to believe that this was going to be a crazy and complicated job. "Can't you just do that yourself?"

Madeline shook her head. "I no longer work for this company so I'm unable to get into the building. And even if I could, I have no idea how to hack anything. The file is called Goldfish and I'm certain that it's somewhere on the boss' personal computer, but it's locked in his office and he changes his password every week."

"So you want us to steal his hard drive?"

She shook her head again. "It's *very* important that he not know I have this information. See, I need it to—"

Xavier raised her hand, interrupting Madeline. "We don't care about the why – we only care about the how much. Now, unfortunately–"

"We'll do it." Burn said quickly.

"You will?" Madeline felt a wave of relief wash over her.

Burn nodded. "Just tell us everything you know about the office and the boss guy, and give us a week to get it done."

"Okay. Shall I email you the details?"

"Sure."

"That's great! I'll get the information to you right away!" Madeline stood up and hurried away, her barely touched tea remaining behind.

Xavier, who had remained silent during the last part of the conversation, turned to her colleague and frowned. The look transformed her face from bright and cheerful to dark and annoyed.

Burn knew what was coming. She took a drink of her tea – a smoky black that had been steeped three times longer than Xavier's peach-mango-white tea – and readied herself for a fight.

"Burn, what the hell is wrong with you?"

"A lot. You'll have to be more specific than that."

"We don't do hacker jobs," Xavier said, carefully emphasizing each word. "We're low-tech, remember?"

Burn shrugged. "We're in a dry spell. We need the money."

"We can do a lot of things, but neither of us knows how to hack. We can't possibly pull this job off."

"I'm sure we can learn. They've got instructions for all sorts of stuff online these days."

"So you're proposing that we learn how to hack into someone's computer within a week?" she said flatly.

Burn smirked. "We've done crazier things."

Xavier could feel her blood-pressure rising to a dangerously high level. She took a few deep breaths and plastered a fake smile on her face that was somehow more terrifying than the frown. "You are completely insane."

Burn sighed. "Look, X, a job we can maybe sorta learn how do is better than no job at all."

"We'll see about that…"

***

Burn took a deep breath and sat down in front of the computer. The room was silent and still – exactly how she preferred rooms to be. She pressed the power button, bringing the computer to life, and suddenly the room was filled with the sound of the fan spinning and the brightness of the screen, the latter of which almost blinded her. When the operating system's musical intro blasted through the speakers, she was reminded of why she normally didn't bother with computers.

Getting into the building had been easy. Usually companies put a lot into security but she suspected that nobody had tried to break into this building before now because their security was a joke. Burn loved getting into places she wasn't supposed to be in.

When the log-in screen appeared, she cracked her knuckles, put her hands on the keyboard and started typing. Pressing 'Enter' with a flourish, she was surprised to be greeted with a flat sound. The log-in screen informed her that the password she'd entered was wrong.

"Dammit," she muttered.

"What's going on?" Xavier's voice asked in her ear.

"Nothing," she replied, wishing that they'd forgone the coms for this job. The last thing she wanted was for Xavier to be proved right.

"Not going as well as you'd expected, MacGyver?" Xavier mocked through the earpiece.

"Wrong reference," she countered. "MacGyver worked with duct tape and paperclips. He never had to hack anything."

"Have you seen every episode? He might have hacked something."

"Have *you* seen every episode? He might *not*."

Xavier laughed. "Are you certain that arguing with me is the most productive use of your time?"

"Shut up."

Xavier laughed again before falling silent.

Burn grit her teeth and tried again to bypass the log-in screen but it was unsuccessful. She wondered how many tries she had before she'd be locked out. If she got locked out then the next time the boss logged in he'd definitely know that someone had been here.

If she was perfectly honest with herself, she had no idea what she was doing – no clue at all. Hacking wasn't as glamorous as the movies made it look or as easy. Since she didn't know what operating system she'd be up against she wasn't able to look up anything specific, and the generic stuff wasn't getting her anywhere. She also didn't know if the information she'd found online was trustworthy or if it had been written by some kid trying to sound awesome by spouting a bunch of crap.

The thought of going back empty handed galled her. There was no guarantee that she'd learn enough to be able to hack the system if she came back a second or even a third time – and as fun as it was to break into places, she hated repetition.

Burn looked around the darkened office. It was much larger than the other offices in the building. There wasn't much furniture – just the desk, a side table, a small couch, and a few chairs. There were no filing cabinets or book-shelves, and only one picture of a sailing boat hung on the wall. Windows lined the wall to her right, the wall to her left contained the door out of the office, and in front of her were the doors to a private bathroom and a small closet. She began to rifle carefully through through the desk, searching for a sticky note that might have the password written on it, but she found nothing. Apparently this guy had a good memory.

"Are you sure I can't just take the computer and run?" she said out loud.

"Nope," Xavier replied. "Our client said that we could leave no trace. A missing computer would definitely be considered traceable."

"But I could bring it back before the start of work to-morrow."

"You mean the start of work *today*? If you can't hack it now, I doubt that you'll be able to do so in five hours."

"Ye of little faith..."

"Ye of big ambition..."

Burn looked around the room again. Her only option was to leave and try again another day. Unless...

"I have an idea," she said.

"I have a bad feeling…"

"Do you remember the Anderson Job?"

"Seriously?"

Burn smiled. "Yeah."

"But do you -"

"I've got my pack."

Xavier's sigh was audible. "Do whatever you want. I'm going to bed."

***

At 8:06am Mr. Ryerson entered his office. He walked over to his closet, hung up his coat, and then went to his desk. He sat down, turned on his computer and logged in.

First he checked his email – his personal account, not the professional. Then he visited a few websites, checking the news and sports highlights, before finally getting to his work email. He locked his computer at 10:22am, when he took a thirty minute break to get coffee and a pastry at the coffee shop one block away. Lunch was from 12:11pm to 1:42pm, during which he locked his computer again before leaving the office. He took another thirty minute break at 3:28pm, coming back to the office with an energy drink and protein bar.

At 4:53pm he left for the day. The rest of the office's employees left shortly afterward, except for a few workers who stayed until 6pm.

***

Xavier looked through her binoculars and into the darkened office. The night vision setting made it possible for her to see that the entire room was still and quiet – as it had been for the past twenty minutes. A glance at her watch told her that it was almost 1:00am.

"Burn?" she said into her com.

There was no answer.

"Burn? Are you asleep? Wake up!"

"Dude, just let me finish this chapter!" was the hostile reply.

Xavier glared at the empty office. "My apologies for interrupting your reading. I wrongly assumed that you'd like to *finish* the job that you're *currently working on*."

Burn muttered something that sounded like 'hardass' before continuing to mutter about how she only needed to read two more pages and it wouldn't take that long, and she was at a really good part in the book by the way.

Many possible responses passed through Xavier's mind but she didn't say any of them. Their partnership was partly maintained by both of them knowing when to shut up. Instead she kept the binoculars to her eyes and watched as one of the ceiling tiles moved away and Burn carefully lowered herself into the office.

Xavier was set up in a hotel across the street from the building in question. The room was more expensive than she would have liked – especially for two nights – but the location was necessary. If they managed to complete this job then they'd be able to pay the hotel bill. If they failed then she'd have to get her hands on a credit card fast or they'd have to ghost. Personally, she was rooting for Burn's idea to succeed.

***

Burn turned on the computer and waited for it to boot up, preparing for the noise and brightness. The notebook beside her had Mr. Ryerson's password written on it multiple times. Every time he'd logged into his computer, Burn had been watching, and now she was certain she had his password – *Rigging!1954*. A smile crossed her face as the computer's desktop appeared. Spying was so much easier than hacking.

"I'm in," she said, knowing that Xavier would be waiting with baited breath for any updates.

"Do you know how to find the file?"

"I know what I'm doing," Burn replied defensively. She was used to Xavier questioning her, and the only reason she put up with it was because Xavier was usually right. After all, she'd failed the hacking part. Luckily Burn knew a sure-fire way to find the file.

She clicked on the 'My Computer' icon and copied the contents of the hard drive onto the flash drive she had with her. As the files copied over, she watched the animated icon fly from one folder to the next, moving her head along with the icon. The timer indicated that this could take a while.

"What's wrong?" Xavier asked after many minutes of silence. "Is it there? Do you have the file?"

"What time is it?" Burn asked, side-stepping the question.

"Almost half-past one."

"I have time. Stop micro-managing."

"If I didn't micro-manage you'd have walked out of the office with the computer under your arm."

"Touché. Despite what you may think, everything's under control. Stop worrying or you'll give yourself grey hairs."

Xavier muttered under her breath how she received no respect and how a headache usually followed every time Burn went off on her own plan, but Burn ignored it and continued watching the animated icons.

***

The flash drive was surprising light for all the information that had been put onto it. It had taken almost an hour for everything to copy over, but Burn had still left the office hours before the first employee would arrive. Xavier was waiting for her in the hotel room with baited breath.

"This is it?" Xavier asked, as Burn handed over the flash drive with a flourish.

Burn smiled. "And then some."

Sighing, Xavier sat down at the desk, put the flash drive into her laptop and looked at the contents. There was almost 40 GB of information on the drive.

"Burn, what did you do?"

She sat down on one of the two queen beds, admiring the softness of the bed and the smoothness of the white sheets. "I didn't want to leave anything behind. I mean, what if the file was renamed or something? But don't worry – I'm sure you'll find the Goldfish in no time."

Xavier stared at the screen in front of her. "I hate you."

"I know," she smiled. "I'm going take advantage of this awesome hotel room and go to sleep now, so feel free to dig through that. You know, my back always goes funny after sleeping in the ceiling. If I'm not awake, feel free to deliver the file to what's-her-name when you find it."

"Madeline," Xavier sighed. "Her name is Madeline."

Burn had already crawled beneath the sheets, closing her eyes. "Whatever."

***

When Burn woke up, Xavier was sitting next to the bed, staring at her with a crazed smile on her face. This had only happened on a few rare occasions – one of which was when they discovered that they were wanted by the police in Bratislava, another when she discovered a box of chocolate bars in their fridge and ate the entire contents.

The look could mean anything from *'we have to get the hell out of here'* to *'this is the best day of my life'*.

"What's going on?" Burn asked carefully, stifling a yawn.

"Would you like to know?" Xavier said, almost bouncing in her chair. "Would you really like to know?"

"You're being stranger than usual – which is saying a lot – so, yes."

Xavier grabbed her arm, dragged her out of bed and over to the computer. "So I found Goldfish and met with Madeline and gave her the file and got our money and everything."

"Good for you."

"I'm not done yet!" She smiled maniacally. "After that I went through the rest of the hard drive and I found something *super interesting*!" she said in a sing-song voice.

"And what was that?" she asked, her interest piqued.

"Well, I discovered a file that had information about a bank account in the Cayman Islands, and since I had the file, I therefore had all the information, which means that I was able to transfer all that money to another account."

Burn went still. "This had better not be a joke."

"It's not!" Xavier beamed, bouncing around in her chair. "I mean, it's not enough for us to retire in Paris, but it's way more than this job pulled in!"

"How much are we talking about, X?" Visions of not having to eat crappy food or stay in terrible hotels just to save a buck danced in her head.

"About fifty thousand! It would have been more, but I saw this special on a Scottish castle and I just couldn't resist!"

Burn's mouth fell open. "You what?"

Xavier sighed wistfully. "I've always wanted my own castle."

The Customer is Always Right

Ramona had been having a terrible day. It started with her alarm not going off and costing her thirty minutes of her carefully scheduled morning routine, forcing her to rush to make it to work on time. Her routine was further disrupted when, in her haste, she spilled coffee on her blouse and had to change her entire outfit. Needless to say, she was not in high spirits when she left her apartment.

The aforementioned incidents resulted in Ramona being late to her work by fourteen minutes, which meant that instead of having fifteen minutes to prepare for a big meeting, she now only had one minute to grab her documents and head to the conference room. Despite her best efforts to appear calm and in control, her frazzled nature poked through at times – rifling through papers to find a certain fact, having to pause to try to remember what point came next, forgetting parts of her carefully planned speech. It was strange enough behaviour for her that her boss made mention of it, and although he tried to play off her demeanour like a joke, Ramona was humiliated.

By the time the meeting finally came to an end the only thing that could make her feel better was the thought of her favourite pick-me-up – a half-caff, two-pump-hazelnut, two-pump-vanilla, skinny mocha latte. Grabbing her purse, Ramona left the office and headed to the cafe on the corner. However, when she reached the cafe, the lineup was almost to the door. Letting out an audible sigh, Ramona braced herself for a long wait. Why was it that every time she wanted a caffeine pick-me-up there were always insanely long lines? Didn't they have enough staff? All she could think about were the minutes she was wasting – minutes that could have been spent working. This line was a waste of her precious time.

When she finally reached the front of the line, she gave her order in an exhausted sigh. The person at the cash register was a trainee – of course there would be a person training at this time of day – nervously wrote down the order and rang her though. Ramona moved to the pickup area, wishing that there was some way to avoid this whole ordering process. If only the person on cash was able to remember who she was and what she liked then this would be so much easier.

After what seemed like hours, the barista finally called out her name. Ramona took her drink and immediately took a sip, eagerly awaiting the warm, delicious drink that was sure to make her day better. Instead, she was greeted not with hazelnut and vanilla, but instead hazelnut and caramel. And just like that the last shreds of her good mood were destroyed.

Looking at the writing on the side of the cup, she could see that it had been written down correctly. It must have been the short girl at the espresso machine who messed it up. Her apron tag said 'Trainee' instead of an actual name – of course there was another trainee working right now – but there was nobody standing around her, making sure she did her job correctly, like there should have been.

Ramona let all of the frustration inside of her rise to the surface. She said very loudly, so that the entire cafe could hear her, "Excuse me, but this isn't the drink I ordered. You've made it wrong."

The girl standing in front of the espresso machine opened her eyes wide. "Oh, no. I'm so sorry. What was it supposed to be?"

An offer to remake the drink would have been enough for some, but right now Ramona didn't want that. She was out for blood.

"I'd like to speak to your manager," she said in a haughty voice, turning away from the girl in the green apron. If she didn't make eye contact then the girl would have no choice but to adhere to her demands.

After a short while Ramona heard someone clear their throat behind her.

"I'm the manager. You asked to see me."

Ramona turned around. She held up the offending drink. "I ordered a half-caff, two-pump-hazelnut, two-pump-vanilla, skinny mocha latte, and that is not what I received. I'm pretty sure I received a decaf full-fat caramel latte!"

The manager took the drink and looked at the writing on the side. "I see. Well, I'll have someone make your drink properly right away."

Ramona shook her head. "That's not good enough! Do you understand the amount of time that I am wasting because of this girl's incompetence? I have a very important job and I can't spend half a day here, waiting for something that I have paid so much money for."

"I can offer you your money back," the manager said.

Ramona shook her head again. "No. I don't care about the money. What I want is for that girl to be fired, so that she never again messes up anyone's order. She's obviously not smart enough to work here."

The girl looked as if she might cry, which brought a terrible satisfaction to Ramona.

"Well..." The manager sighed. "Sorry, Jane, but I have to fire you."

The girl's mouth dropped open. "What?"

"You heard the customer – I have to fire you. The customer is always right."

The terrible satisfaction within Ramona increased. She had asked for employees to be fired many times before, but never had the manager actually gone through with it. This was a golden opportunity and Ramona was going to bask in this glory.

Jane frowned and took off her green apron, handing it to the manager.

"Wait for me in my office and we'll start the paperwork."

Jane obediently headed into the back.

The manager turned to Ramona. Ramona was hoping that she'd offer to make her drink again, because she really did want that drink, but instead the manager held out the green apron. Ramona regarded it curiously, wondering if maybe she was offering it to her as a trophy.

"Well, get to it," the manager said.

"Excuse me?"

"I can't operate this cafe without a full staff, and since you made me fire an employee you'll have to take her place. So put the apron on and get behind the counter."

"But..." Ramona couldn't believe what was happening. "But I have a real job."

"You think this job isn't real?" The manager laughed. "Try telling that to everyone behind that counter and everyone waiting in line." She pushed the apron closer to Ramona. "Now put the apron on and get to work. Considering how your tantrum has held everything up, you'd better get a move on. It's a good thing you know everything there is to know about making drinks."

For some strange reason, Ramona found herself taking hold of the apron and putting it on, the fluorescent lights glinting off the 'Trainee' badge. She stepped behind the counter, her eyes wide with confusion. The espresso machine in front of her seemed to grow larger, dwarfing her in its presence. Never before had she felt so small.

Ramona looked at the line-up of cups, all for drinks waiting to be made. Then she looked up at the line of people waiting impatiently for their drinks. A terrifying fear gripped her heart.

Sight

The Poltergeist had been with them for as long as anyone could remember. When the owners of The Ship's Galley Restaurant purchased the building they knew that it had been built over an old graveyard, but also that the bodies had supposedly all been moved. At first they didn't have much trouble with the spirits that began manifesting throughout the building, but those spirits were mostly curious about what was going on above their final resting place.

There had been incidents with items being misplaced or disappearing and showing up in strange areas, but it had been relatively harmless. Ten years ago the incidents began to increase, but they always had an edge of playfulness about them. It was as though the poltergeist had grown bolder and wanted to have some fun.

Then, a few years ago, he changed again. He stopped being so playful and his incidents turned darker. Dishes were breaking, objects were thrown around, and a couple staff members had been injured. Many people quit The Galley for fear of their own safety. Some stuck around, keeping to the buddy system and swearing never to go anywhere alone. Meanwhile, the owners tried everything to stop the incidents and bring about peace, but to no success.

"I hope it works this time," Sandy commented as she

shined the silverware. Over the past three months the owners had brought in two mediums to exorcise the spirit, but still the poltergeist remained. "I'd hate to have to quit on Darren and Judy."

"I know what you mean," Emily replied. She'd been working at The Galley for four years and aside from the poltergeist everything was great. As much as she liked working here, she'd had a few close calls with flying objects and some days it didn't seem worth it. The medium coming in today claimed that she was the real thing, but Emily had long ago grown doubtful of those claiming to have the 'second sight'.

"Ten minutes until she arrives," Sandy said, looking at the clock. The medium was scheduled to arrive at 3pm, between the lunch and supper rush. The 'exorcism' was supposed to take between 25 and 45 minutes and should ride them of the spirit for good. They never bothered naming the poltergeist. Most of the ideas they came up with had quickly been replaced with terms like 'Jerk' and 'Nuisance'. Nobody really cared about his background. Either he was angry about losing his peaceful resting place or he was an unsatisfied customer come back to haunt them. No matter what story they came up with, it wouldn't stop him for throwing plates at the waiters.

The restaurant was almost empty except for a middle-aged man sitting alone at a table and a group of four ghost-hunting teenagers. The teenagers were more concerned about seeing a ghost than their meals, while the man was quietly drinking a cup of coffee after having a late lunch.

"Should we ask them to go?" Emily said, looking at the five customers.

"Probably not. I doubt those four would agree to go

anywhere once they realize what's about to happen."

The medium was five minutes late and was wearing something that looked like a 'Psychic' Halloween costume. She was covered in scarves and skirts and held her hands in weird positions. Emily instantly took a dislike to her. The woman looked like she was trying too hard.

"My name is Matilda Moondrop," the medium said. "Now, where is your pesky ghost?"

Darren and Judy gave her a tour of the restaurant, pointing out the places where he acted up the most. When they were back at the middle of the dining room, Matilda stopped them.

"Oh, yes!" she proclaimed loudly. "His energy is very strong here!"

Emily noticed that the man sitting alone smiled and shook his head. She fought the urge to do the same.

Matilda raised her hands to the sky. "My friend, I know that you are greatly tormented and this is why you lash out at others, but you are among friends here. Please, show us a sign that you understand."

A saucer flew past the medium, almost hitting her.

She gasped before quickly collecting herself. "He communicates in the only way he knows," Matilda said. "We understand you, my friend, and we want you to be happy and at peace."

While she flailed around the dining room, the man looked away from her and at the ghostly specter standing to the left of the group. The ghost was looking at the medium with an exasperated expression and was obviously ready to throw something else.

"Don't deny yourself eternal rest, my friend!" Matilda wailed as she raised her hands to the sky and shook them frantically. "Go towards the light! Go towards the light!"

The ghost turned to grab something, but as he moved he noticed the man staring at him. The ghost looked around, wondering if there was something around him, but the man was definitely looking at him. He ignored the wails of the crazy lady in the skirts and walked over to the man's table.

"I see Him!" Matilda continued. "He's starting to go! He's looking at the light! He understands that eternal peace lies within and he feels so weary and tired! He wants to be at peace and rest!"

Emily fought back the urge to sigh. She'd seen so many mediums do and say the same thing. She turned around and looked at the customers. The four teenagers were completely engrossed in Matilda's performance, but the attention of the old man was elsewhere. In fact, it almost looked like he was talking to someone, but there was nobody sitting in the chair across from him.

"Oh yes!" Matilda exclaimed, shaking her hands even more. "He's going into the light! He's leaving us! He's going to a better place! He's going!" She held her arms rigid, stretching them as high as they would go. Then she suddenly collapsed to the floor, breathing heavily. Everyone but Emily rushed to her side.

Discreetly, Emily looked over at the man. He was still talking with his unseen companion. The man smiled and nodded his head, and then went back to his coffee.

Matilda had risen to her feet by now, explaining to everyone how drained she was and how much energy it had taken to lure the spirit towards the light. Nothing had been thrown since the first saucer and people were beginning to wonder if it had actually worked.

After Matilda had sat down and drank a cup of tea to calm her nerves, she said that it was time to take her leave. Darren and Judy paid her and escorted her out of the restaurant.

"That was pretty intense," Sandy said when Matilda was gone. "I wonder if it actually worked this time."

"Maybe," Emily said, looking over at the man. He caught her staring at him and gave her a smile.

"It would be great if the spirit was finally gone," Sandy continued. "I'd love to work without dodging dishes all day long. Although I have my doubts about that medium..."

"I guess we'll see," Emily replied before excusing herself. She walked over to the man's table. "Would you like a refill, sir?" she asked, looking at his empty coffee cup.

"No thank you," he replied. "That will be all. For myself and for Edward, as well."

She raised an eyebrow inquisitively.

"As long as you don't bring in any more false mediums who run about the place yelling their heads off, he should behave. And if he doesn't behave," he took out a business card and placed it on the table, "you have my number. Now, would you be so kind to bring me my bill?"

Emily smiled. "You know what, it's on the house."

Only a Story

Jack was an idiot.

He was constantly telling stupid stories about amazing things that he'd supposedly done. We all knew he was lying, but nobody had the heart to call him out. Instead, we played along.

Yes, Jack, we totally believe that you sold a cow for some beans. And not just any beans, but magic beans. Yes, that's something a sane person who's on the edge of starvation would do.

We absolutely *believe that those beans grew into a giant beanstalk that nobody else in the village could see. And that you climbed it up into the sky and found a land of giants who lived on clouds. Sounds* perfectly *plausible.*

Don't even get me started on the goose or the harp…

Nobody cared for Jack's stories, but he never stopped sharing, letting them grow grander with each re-telling. We learned to tune him out and never question him.

Jack was an idiot, and everyone in the village knew.

But there was one strange green tree within the forest that seemed to be impossibly tall. It was merely a trick of the light or an odd angle. It couldn't possibly go all the way up into the clouds.

And if one were to climb that tree, there was no way that they'd find a land where items were ten times their normal size, where giants roamed and great treasures lay.

Giants and elves and magic weren't real, after all.
It was only a story.

THRILLER

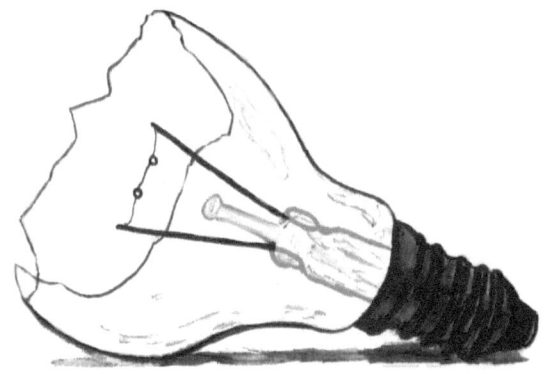

The Taste of Copper

When I was three years old, my mother showed me how to place a copper penny on my tongue and hold it still for one minute. It was something the two of us shared – a ritual we did every single night before bed. She told me that it kept the bad dreams away, and I have to admit that I can't remember ever having a bad dream as a child.

As I grew older, I learned that the other children in the city didn't have the same night-time ritual. When I asked my mother why nobody else did this, she simply said that our family was different. At first she was reluctant to tell the whole story, but I pushed until she gave in.

After hearing it, I wished that I had never asked.

Long ago, when my grandmother was a young child, she lived in a small village on the coast. The village has since been abandoned due to resettlement, but if you decided to go there now you would see the remnants of houses and graveyards, silent and waiting.

One winter's evening, when my grandmother was very young, word spread from a nearby town that there was a strange woman in the area. It was odd for a person to be wandering at night, especially in winter, and the townsfolk wondered if the woman might be a witch or a demon. They hid themselves in their homes, locking the doors and turning off the lights, hoping that the stranger would think the town was abandoned and pass by.

Eventually they heard a hacking cough making its way into the town. Those that chanced a look saw an old woman dressed in dark rags, using a tall branch as a walking stick. Every so often her body would be wracked with that terrible cough, doubling her over in pain. She slowly shuffled through the town, taking in the dark houses.

It was the snow that gave them away, showing the footsteps of earlier journeys throughout the town, stopping at buildings that seemed abandoned but were too nice and well kept. The woman began knocking on doors and windows, begging with her rasping voice for food and shelter, but the townspeople stayed quiet. They knew how evil spirits pretended to be helpless, to make unsuspecting people invite them in. They would not risk such things.

The woman knocked on every door, shouting that she knew they were inside, but the townsfolk were paralyzed with fear and prayed that she would leave them in peace. Eventually she left the town, but not before laying her curse:

You people have no mercy, but you will not forget me so easily. If you love your pennies so dearly, keep them. But rest assured that one day you will all know what it is to feel an emptiness in your stomach and coldness in your bones. One day you will all know how it feels to be helpless.

And then she disappeared into the night.

The townspeople wondered if they had done the right thing, if maybe she had been nothing more than an old woman after all, but they all agreed that letting her into the village would have brought disease and sickness. They had done the right thing.

A few days later, a group of men who were out hunting found her body. They were unsure whether she had died of starvation, the elements, or her illness. They buried her in a shallow, unmarked grave and tried to forget about all the unpleasantness the woman's visit had brought.

Everything returned to normal, but after a while the townspeople noticed that something was wrong with their food. No matter what they ate, everything tasted bitter and rotten. Even food that was fresh or brought in from other towns had the same taste. Some whispered that it was the curse, come to torment them for turning the strange woman away. Others were sceptical, but there was no logical explanation for what was happening.

Every man, woman, and child in the town began to starve, unable to keep food in their stomachs. As they wasted away, a chill crept through their bodies, the likes of which they had never felt before, not even on the coldest nights of the year.

Thankfully a solution was found before too many perished. Remembering the stranger's words about keeping their pennies to themselves, a woman decided to put a penny in her mouth. After a minute she found that the rotten taste had given way to the copper of the coin, and she was able to eat again. She spread the word to everyone and the village was saved.

My mother explained that this curse did not stop with those who had lived in the village, but travelled to their offspring as well. She and her brothers and sisters were affected by the curse, while my father, who was from another town, was not. So every night I had to place a copper penny under my tongue to keep the curse away.

I was young enough to trust her implicitly. I believed every word and followed every instruction. But then I grew up, and I began to question her story.

Why would someone curse an entire town for not

helping? Did she curse any other towns or was this one special? Were curses even real? And if they were, why would it affect me – someone who was born decades after this had happened? Would it pass on to my kids, if I had any? Were pennies made of copper anymore?

Doubts filled my mind. I was a rational, educated person, and this story went against everything I believed. So one night I decided that I would not do my nightly ritual. I was haunted by bad dreams, but I had expected as much. With the story of the curse foremost in my mind, it was bound to manifest as nightmares. The next day I was able to eat just fine, so again I did not put a penny under my tongue. Nothing bad happened. The curse was no more – if it had even existed in the first place.

Eight days later it started. No matter what I tried to eat, everything had a stale, unpleasant taste to it, as if it had been left sitting in the elements for years. Every drink, even water, tasted rotten and bitter. I knew that I needed food to live, but the thought of eating repulsed me. Whenever I tried to keep anything in my stomach, I would have to fight to stop it from coming back up – a fight that I would often lose. Days passed and I noticed how thin my arms and legs were getting, and how hollow my face looked. My energy was waning, and I could feel a chill inside of me that I had never felt before. It felt as if someone had replaced my blood and bones with ice, and no matter how many sweaters I worse, I couldn't make the chill go away.

I refused to believe that this was the curse. There had to be a realistic explanation, like a dormant illness. I went to a doctor, but he could find no reason why this was happening and suggested that I go a psychiatrist, as it was probably all in my mind. I never went. If this was my mind playing tricks, then it would have happened right after I stopped using the penny, not days after. No, this was something more – something inexplicable.

I still don't know if I truly believe in the curse, but I can think of no other explanation. Perhaps it is too late, perhaps I have left it too long, but it is the only hope I have left. So I will take this penny and place it on my tongue, and I will keep it there until the curse has broken. I don't know how long this will take, or if the curse will break my spirit before I break it, but I can only hope that I will survive long enough to once more know the taste of copper.

The Deal

Claire had been prepared to make a sacrifice. She had heard many stories about people who sought out the witch for a favour and never returned, but those stories also claimed that every favour asked for was granted. One man wanted help for his poor family, and although he never returned home, his family became very wealthy the next day. One woman went to seek revenge on a man who had deceived her, and though she was never seen or heard from again, the man was trampled to death by horses a few days later.

When her sister fell ill, Claire tried desperately to bring her back to health, but as her sister grew weaker and weaker, she knew that there was only one option left. She had been prepared to give her life in exchange, so when the witch offered to cure her sister in return for one month's servitude, Claire was more than happy to accept. Perhaps the witch had taken pity on her, she wondered, and given her an easy task.

The terms were that Claire had to keep house for the witch, performing any possible task that was given to her, and that she would not leave the witch's forest until after the thirty-first sunrise. Claire shook the witch's small, bony hand in agreement. The witch grinned and declared that Claire's sister would be in full health by the morning.

The work was harder than Claire had expected. She had to cook, clean, maintain the grounds and the garden, and do any other task the witch came up with. Some days she would spend hours putting things in order only to find a mess the next day. The witch only gave her a few minutes to eat or rest, keeping her constantly moving. Some days Claire thought about running away, but then she remembered her promise to the witch. Claire thought of her sister and how wonderful it would be to return home once her time had been served.

The only time the witch took pity on her was when she slept. After working twelve gruelling hours, Claire would go back to her small room within the witch's house. There she would mark a line on the wall, to count down the days that had passed, before falling asleep, exhausted, while the sun was still in the sky.

The witch's forest was quite different from the forest that surrounded her village. The trees were all a sickly grey colour and had no leaves or pine, just bare gnarled branches. She didn't like when a task took her into the forest, and tried to spend as little time in there as possible. The wind made it seem as though the trees were whispering to her, mocking her. The grass was brown and dry, making the green of the gardens seem unnatural.

She saw no other living thing, except for the witch. There weren't even any animals or bugs. Any questionable creatures or objects in the house were already dead. Claire had wondered if she would see any of the other people who had come to ask favours, but there was nobody but her, the witch, and the trees.

Finally her thirtieth day came and Claire arose to a bright morning. The sun filtered through the branches much the same as it had any other day, but today it seemed brighter. She couldn't help smiling as she walked out to the kitchen, receiving her duties from the witch. Only one more day and she would finally be home, back where she belonged. The task had been difficult, but it would be worth it to see her sister's healthy, smiling face.

After finishing her chores, Claire was exhausted, but decided to stay awake all night and watch the sunrise. She made herself a cup of strong tea and sat outside, watching the sky. She thought about all the wonderful things that she would do once she was back home, the people she missed, the places she would visit, and the food she would eat.

Suddenly she noticed that the sun hadn't set. She had been sitting outside for a long time, but the sky was just as bright. A terrible idea started to form in her mind, but she ignored it and went into the house, checking on the small clock the witch kept in the kitchen. The clock proclaimed that it was almost midnight, and yet the sun was high in the sky.

"Problem?" the witch asked.

Claire turned around, startled by her sudden appearance. "The clock says that it is midnight, but the sun is still up."

The witch smiled. "That clock goes by village time, dear."

"Village time?" She shook her head, confused. "But there is only one time."

"Is there?"

Claire felt the terrible idea start to form again, but she shook it off. "I have been here for thirty days, and in the morning, I will go home."

"Our agreement was that you would leave when the sun rose for the thirty-first time. How can a sun rise if it does not set?"

Dread washed over her. "You cannot..."

The witch smiled wickedly. "If I recall correctly, the sun has not set since your arrival. Hence, you cannot leave."

Claire raced outside and looked at the sky. The sun was still shining through the branches, showing no signs of wanting to set. She tried to think of a time when she had noticed darkness in the forest, but there was only sunlight.

"Don't worry, dear," the witch's voice was suddenly behind her. "The sun will set after another hundred hours or so, and then the night will come. You'll learn the timing soon enough."

Claire thought back to the past thirty days she had spent toiling in the witch's house and how it had not even measured up to one sunrise. This could not be. How could the sun not set or rise here? How could one day last almost a thousand hours? Did the witch have control over the sun or was this some kind of illusion meant to keep her here until the end of time?

Who knew how long the nights would last or if the sun would even rise again? If this were the case, she would die of old age before she could leave.

"No," she said aloud. "A day is made up of twenty-four hours. I have worked my thirty days, and in the morning I will leave."

"If that is what you think, dear." The witch laughed to herself and went back into the house.

Claire stared at the sunlight filtering in through the trees. She spent hours waiting for the sky to change, but it didn't. Finally she went back into the house and checked the clock. It was eight am, well past sunrise in the actual world.

"Has the sun finally risen?" The witch's words came out of nowhere.

Claire turned around, but the witch was nowhere to be seen. As she looked around the room, the witch began to laugh. Her laughter grew louder and more terrifying, and soon it filled the entire house. Claire put her hands over her ears, but the sound couldn't be shut out. She ran from the house, into the ever-present daylight and raced through the trees.

The trees seemed to have grown extra branches, blocking every path she chose. Branches scraped at her skin, cutting her as if they were blades. The whispering of the wind grew louder until it sounded like soft voices telling her to give up – that there was no escape.

Finally she could see the clearing that led to the village and her home. In her heart she knew that she was right – that she had served her time and should be allowed to leave – and she raced forward.

With each step the ground seemed to grow softer, and her feet sank deeper the further she ran. Her right foot sank into the ground and refused to come free, no matter how hard she pulled. The clearing was less than twenty feet away, and she grabbed her foot, trying to pull it free. It was then that she noticed the skin on her arms had turned a sickly grey colour. Panic rose inside her as she tried to pull her foot from the ground, but the ground was growing around her foot, encasing her leg. She reached for a tree to help pull herself forward, but her arms and fingers began to grow longer and she couldn't grab anything.

Frantically, Claire looked around for help, but all she could see were the grey trees. As tears filled her eyes, she began to see that there were souls trapped inside the trees

– the souls of humans who had dared to seek out the witch and ask for a favour – staring at her with pain and regret in their eyes. She tried to yell that she had served her time and that she was free to go, but her mouth wouldn't open.

The other trees watched silently as the transformation finished, and the woods fell silent again.

Usurper

There are strange things brewing up in the world. Things that should only be found in the imaginations of the deeply disturbed; that should not exist. The boogeyman was never supposed to be real, but the fear was. The fear is always real.

It doesn't help that the caste system is a bitch. Once you're in you can't get out, no matter how hard you try. Fancy tales of servant girls marrying princes – that kind of thing don't happen in real life. Maybe the prince'll bed you, but he sure as hell ain't gonna marry you, no matter what he says when he's lying 'twist your thighs.

You need a job, food, clothes, a roof over your head – so what are you going to do? You're pretty enough. Don't want to turn your hands blue in a dyehouse or ruin that smooth skin in a launderette. Certainly don't wanna marry some old man who'll use you like a whore and give you a brood of bratty kids you can't afford to feed. Might as well be a proper whore. At least you'll have your freedom.

But what about the men you've got to deal with? The kinds of men who go for whores ain't exactly the best men in town. Sure some of 'em are princes, but at long as you can make each and every one of 'em feel like a king it'll be all right. Just give it five minutes and he'll be gone – and the next king-to-be's all ready waiting.

Then you hear there's a usurper in town. But he

don't want the kings, no. He wants the ones who make the kings. And he's beautiful, they say, a right handsome man. A nice face to stare at whilst he slits your throat and bleeds you dry.

Screaming won't do you any good with no breath to draw in. Even if you could scream, who'd come to help the likes of you? Who's stupid enough to go running down a dark street to help some whore? Everyone knows when you hear a scream at night you walk the other way.

You never heard no yelling last night, but if you had you'd have turned away. Ain't safe for a lady to be barging into dangerous areas late at night. You'd never have been able to help her, anyways – would have got yourself sliced up along with her, and you don't want that.

The dark streets were your home but now they're looking more like your tomb. A labyrinth for you to run through until you finally get caught by the Minotaur. And boy how terrifying he is – and what big, sharp horns he has.

What's a working girl to do? Can't quit. Can't make money just sitting around. Gotta eat, gotta drink, gotta work.

Besides, you tell yourself, maybe she had it coming. Maybe she acted the fool or said the wrong thing or tried to rip him off. Can't go cheating your customers – at least not the ones who won't be cheated. You, you're smarter than that. You knows better, you do. You're a careful girl.

So you dust off your petticoats and go to work.

It's a quiet night. The usurper's probably gone by now – long gone. Halfway to Norfolk by now. Wouldn't bother hanging around here – no, he'd be caught for sure. Can't just commit murder and expect to get away with it.

Tonight you make kings.

Tonight you're safe.

But tomorrow there's another girl, another whore trapped in the labyrinth. The usurper strikes again. They say he did things to her – horrible things. Used a knife as sharp as his his smile. His eyes sparkle, they say, as he cuts you open and plays with your insides.

It's a game to him. And he always wins. You might not want to play, but you got no choice. The choice is all up to him.

But a girl's gotta earn a living. Can't stay home all night, hiding under the covers. Won't get paid for that. Keep telling yourself that you'll be safe, that he'll leave the town, but the days pass and the bodies pile up. More kingmakers dead.

The usurper seems to like it here. Ain't gonna go until his business is done.

You get nervous about work – looking over your shoulder all the time, peering into shadows. Nice looking guy comes over and you turn away. Can't risk losing your head. Stick to the ugly, homely guys and maybe you'll stay alive.

Standing on the street you're feeling colder tonight than you ever felt – and it ain't got nothing to do with the weather. Cold chill going through you today, just like yesterday and the day before.

All you needs is a few coins to get you through the night. Get some food, drink, a place to sleep that's got a bit of heat. One customer's all you need, but that customer's not here. Your stomach's aching for food. Can't turn back now or you'll be starved to death before sunrise.

And then you see him – a potential customer. The lighting ain't the best, but you can see as he gets closer – he's good looking. A nice face to stare at...

But this can't be him – can't be the killer of king-makers. Look at his smile, it's too nice for a murderer. He's got one thing on his mind and it ain't blood.

Could turn him away, but who knows when the next man's going to come by. You need the coins. Gonna starve to death if you don't make some money – might get stabbed to death if you go with the handsome stranger. Knife or starvation? Which one sounds better?

Besides, maybe this ain't him. You've slept with hundreds of men and none of them have tried to kill you yet. You're a careful girl.

And surely this ain't your last night on Earth. Is God really gonna let you die with your old petticoats on and an empty stomach? Without a chance to wash your hair and dress up a little?

You think you'd be able to sense it if it was your last night alive.

So you think of the coins and you take his hand...

The Vicious Ones

Once upon a time, many centuries ago, our clan lived in harmony with the Vicious Ones. They had a different name back then, back in the peaceful days, but it has been lost to time. While they were not as advanced as we, we watched them grow over the years, learning how to adapt to this world. They were aware of our existence, as we were of theirs, but we kept to our own clans, existing side-by-side in harmony.

But one day those within our clan began to disappear. We stopped hearing their voices in our head, finding only silence when we searched them out. Our clan realized that something terrible was going on, and sent out warnings about the new, unknown danger, putting everyone on alert.

Eventually one of our clan was able to send us an image of a Vicious One descending on them before the image disappeared and there was only darkness. We never heard from that clan member again.

It was our nature to be peaceful and seek resolve without violence. We tried to communicate with the Vicious Ones, to ask why they were doing this, but they were not evolved enough to understand our language. Or maybe they did hear our thoughts but were too wicked to care.

Some talked of fighting back, but we knew that using physical violence would damn our souls to the Eternal

Darkness. So we continued with our futile plan of trying to make these evil creatures understand our pain, hoping that one day we would be heard and they would end their reign of terror. We knew that any moment we might be taken away, yet still we dared to live.

Then the Vicious Ones came for me, wrenching me from my home and severing my link to the rest of the clan. Where once I heard a multitude of voices in my head, there was now silence and despair. I was put into darkness, and taken far away from my home. We had often wondered what the Vicious Ones did with those they captured. The answer was more disturbing than I could have imagined.

As I stared at the sharp knife before me, I tried to project my thoughts into the creature standing before me. I tried to tell them how beautiful life was, how I loved my family and friends, and how they had taken me from a life that I was not ready to leave, but they did not listen.

As the knife sliced into my flesh, I could see tears form in the eyes of my tormenter. I wondered if my message had reached them, if they would realize their mistake and let me go, but my hopes were dashed as they raised the knife again. Tears began to fall from their eyes as another slice cut into me, and I realized that I could only send my emotions and nothing else.

My tormentor cried, but they did not understand why…

Beneath the Ice

She disappeared during the storm.

Outside their small, isolated home the blizzard raged, but inside he was the one raging. She'd pleaded, saying there was more than enough firewood to last the night and offering to get more once the storm had calmed, but in his drunken rage he refused to listen.

While she reluctantly headed outside he continued to drink himself senseless, and when he awoke the next morning she was nowhere to be found.

Outside, everything was covered in a blanket of thick white snow. There was no sign of her anywhere.

Suddenly he heard a tapping. He followed it onto the frozen lake, walking carefully on the slippery ice. At the centre of the lake, where the tapping was the loudest, he wiped the snow away. She was trapped underneath the ice – her skin white and lips blue. Her eyes pleaded with him to rescue her.

Guilt overwhelmed him. Her fate was his fault, but maybe it wasn't too late. He smashed at the ice desperately with his fist. Her eyes continued to plead as he slammed his fist again and again, staining the ice red with his blood.

When he finally broke through, he reached into the frigid water, but she was gone. Frantically, he cleared off more snow, but she was nowhere to be found.

Sitting back, he took a few deep breaths to calm himself. Perhaps he'd imagined it. Perhaps it wasn't real.

Suddenly he felt a cold, wet hand on his shoulder.

The Inevitable

Most nights Hannah didn't dream. She'd close her eyes, try to clear her mind, and the next thing she'd know daylight would be streaming in through her window. When she mentioned it to her parents they told her that some people just don't dream, and that it wasn't anything to feel strange about, so it never bothered her.

However, on the rare occasions that she actually dreamed, it would always be the same thing. She would be standing somewhere, all alone. Then she would feel it – deep inside her, something aching to be set free. Her heart would start to race and the power would surge within her, running through her veins, along her entire body. She was invincible. With one thought she could burn down buildings and destroy towns.

But then she'd wake up and she'd return to ordinary, average Hannah.

She never told anyone about those dreams, not even her parents. In her small town she already felt like an outcast, being the only adopted child in her high school. It might have been easier for her if she looked like her parents, but in every family photo her dark features stood out like a sore thumb against their fair hair and skin. She knew that they loved her, but it didn't stop her from feeling like an outsider. It didn't help that the entire town was strangely singular. Most children looked exactly like their parents and those who didn't were the 'troubled children', the black sheep of the family who wanted to stand out.

"Hannah, it's time for breakfast!" her mother called out from downstairs, her voice waking Hannah from the dream just as she was about to let the power loose from her hands.

Sighing, Hannah pushed back the covers and got out of bed. Her pink plaid pyjamas matched the room perfectly. Everything was white and pink, with a white wicker bed, vanity, and chair. Her bedspread and curtains were pink, three shades darker than the colour of her walls. Her mother didn't like clutter, so she kept her posters and nick-nacks in the closet, tucked away. The room had been designed by her mother and was the perfect girl's room for the perfect girl.

Slipping her feet into a pair of fuzzy pink slippers, Hannah obediently headed downstairs to the kitchen. Her parents believed in early rising, even on the weekends. She would have loved another hour to two of sleep, but she never said anything.

As she entered the kitchen, her mother greeted her with a big smile. "Are you excited for today?"

She paused, confused, but then she remembered. Today was the harvest festival. It was usually a fun time with lots of games and rides and fairground foods, but that wasn't what her mother was talking about. Plastering a smile on her face, she nodded. "Yes, mother. I am."

"I'm glad to hear that. Just be sure to behave yourself. I'd hate to hear anyone in the town talking about you doing anything inappropriate at the festival."

"Yes, mother."

Her mother placed a plate of eggs and toast in front of her and she dug in, hoping that nothing else would be said about the festival. The truth was that she wasn't excited, not at all. Normally she would be, but this time she wasn't going with her friends. Instead she was going with Austin Henderson. On a date.

Austin lived down the street and her parents knew his parents, and they'd been friends since they were young. Every time her mother mentioned his name Hannah knew that she was dreaming of the two of them getting married. The problem was that Hannah didn't want to marry Austin. He was always kind to her and was a great friend, but she had her eye on someone else. Unfortunately she doubted that her parents would approve of her choice.

During breakfast her father said very little, spending most of his time making subtle noises to himself as he read the newspaper while her mother continued to talk excitedly. Normally her mother thought of the festival as a time where kids were encouraged to run around and act impulsively, but today it seemed that today her mother had nothing but good things to say.

Finishing her food, Hannah excused herself from the table and headed upstairs to get ready. Austin wouldn't be picking her up for another two hours, but she wanted to take a long shower and prepare herself for what was surely going to be a weird day. She shouldn't have agreed to the date, but she knew that it was what her parents wanted. If her mother found out that Austin had asked her out and she'd said no, Hannah would never hear the end of it. She wished that she had some kind of actual power, like in her dreams. If she could make it rain, then the festival would be cancelled and so would the date. But this was real life and things like that didn't exist out here.

After her shower, she saw that her mother had come into her room and laid out a pink dress and white cardigan for her to wear. She'd rather wear jeans and a sweater – actually she'd rather wear anything but pink – but if she walked out of the house wearing something other than this dress, her mother would frown and fret all day.

Sighing, she obediently dressed in the outfit her mother had set out. Then she sat at her vanity and stared at her face in the mirror. Although it was her face she didn't feel much like herself. She loved her parents and wanted them to be proud of her, but as she grew older, it was getting more and more difficult to align her own hopes and dreams with those of her parents. She tied her long black hair into a ponytail and put on some pink lip gloss. She could do this, she reassured herself. She just had to take it one day at a time.

A few seconds later her mother knocked on the door, opening it before Hannah had a chance to say anything. "Austin's here, sweetie. Are you ready?"

"Yes," she said, smiling as she stood up.

Her mother's smile disappeared as her lips tightened. She took in Hannah's outfit, carefully examining each part. "Are you sure you wouldn't rather wear your hair down? I could curl it for you."

"I'd hate to make Austin wait," she replied. "Besides, it might be windy out, and I wouldn't want it getting in my eyes."

Her practical counter-point made her mother concede. Practicality always outweighed romanticism in this house. Hannah wondered if there was a way to practically argue why she should wear jeans instead, but she had a feeling that her mother wouldn't give up so easily on that one.

Hannah walked downstairs to meet Austin, who was trying and failing to hide his nervousness. He kept using his right hand to press down his brown hair, which was already flattened to his head. He was also dressed for the occasion, with a light blue button-up shirt and coffee-coloured pants. Hannah cringed inwardly. Anyone who looked at them would have no doubt that they were on a date.

Fending off her mother's request for pictures, she said a quick goodbye and hurried Austin out the front door.

The walk to the festival grounds was awkward. Ever since she'd realized that Austin liked her, she'd notice how awkward he could be around her. It wasn't a bother because she had no romantic ideals towards him and he didn't push the subject, but then he'd had to go and ask her on a date and ruin it. The mood was dramatically different now. It was awkward – completely and utterly awkward. He was no longer a friend – now he was a weight of expectation around her neck – a ring and a future that she didn't want but didn't know how to say no to.

They tried to talk as they walked to the fair grounds, discussing classes and assignments, but the conversation no longer flowed easily. Hannah found that she was talking strangely, her voice louder than normal and her sentences short, stumbling over words she'd said a hundred times. She was painfully aware of how close or far they were from each other at all times. At one point she glanced at Austin and could see by the slightly pained look on his face that he too felt this was weird.

A small devil on her shoulder wondered if she should try to sabotage this date, if she should make Austin think that she was utterly un-marryable so that he'd stop thinking of her and move on to someone else. Surely her parents would understand that. Giving herself a mental shake, she realized two things – one: her parents would find out that the dissolution of their dreams was her fault and would blame themselves for not raising her better; and two: she couldn't be mean to Austin, no matter how much she didn't want to marry him.

The angel on her other shoulder told her that she might as well make the best of today. After all, they'd been to the festival before as friends and had fun, so there was no reason they couldn't have fun today. Switching gears, she ignored their outfits and the press of her parent's expectations and tried to imagine that they were two pals hanging out. It didn't completely work, but it helped a little.

Once they reached the festival they wandered through the exhibits, going through the petting zoo, feeding goats, and looking at the peacocks that farmer Johnson owned. Occasionally they would run into friends of theirs, who never asked to join them and always left them alone after a quick chat. Hannah could see that other people were taking notice of Austin and her, mostly other parents who smiled and whispered to each other. It was starting to drive her crazy but then Austin suggested playing some of the games and she was able to focus her energy on that. She was more academic than sporty, so even though she tried her hardest she always lost. Austin wasn't very skilled at sports either, but he was strong due to his work on the farm and ended up winning her a teddy bear by knocking over milk bottles with a baseball. He picked a purple bear for her out of the selection of multi-coloured prizes, and as she took hold of the soft toy she felt a blush start to creep up into her cheeks. Most people would think that pink was her favourite colour because of how her mother dressed her, but Austin remembered that purple was her favourite.

"Hey," Austin said suddenly, "we haven't done any rides yet. We should go on the Ferris wheel."

Hannah didn't trust her voice, so she nodded and followed him. As they walked, Austin talked about the game and how they set up the milk bottles in a way that they were supposed to be difficult to knock over, but he'd played the game every year at the festival, so he knew the secret. She half-listened, allowing her thoughts to wander.

She thought about how her life was structured to be her parent's perfect daughter and how in order for her to try to fight it and rebel she would need a strength she knew she didn't have. If she wanted to live her own life then she'd likely have to do it alone and that scared her. What if she gave everything up and never found happiness? What if she lived the rest of her life regretting her decisions? At least if she married Austin she'd still have her friends and family. Would it be so terrible to marry him? He was nice to her, and she couldn't imagine him ever treating her badly. Although she liked someone else there was no guarantee that her crush felt the same. Asking the question would likely result in a terrible heartbreak, especially in a town like this. With Austin she knew exactly what she was getting.

She'd thought she had a choice in the matter but it suddenly became clear that she didn't.

Snapping back into reality, she saw that they were near the front of the line. Austin was still jabbering on about how all the games here were fixed.

"I see," she said gently, hoping that he'd get the hint to stop.

He stopped talking and nodded.

They reached the front of the line and were moved into one of the seats. It was a small enough bench that they were almost touching. As the attendant brought the safety bar down over them Hannah wondered just how safe these contraptions were. It was the exact same ride from her childhood, but although it had seemed sturdy and secure then, she now realized that they were being held aloft by nuts and bolts. She tried to reassure herself by saying that they had to test these things before allowing anyone on them.

Austin cleared his throat as the Ferris wheel climbed upwards. "I know that you'd rather be here with your friends, but I'm glad you agreed to come out with me. I know that your parents really wanted you to do this, but I hope that there was a part of you-"

"Austin," she interrupted, "I'm having a good time. Honest. Don't worry about it."

He gave her a half-smile but she could tell he wasn't convinced.

The wheel finished its second full revolve and continued upward. Once they were a few chairs away from the bottom, it stopped to let off passengers and let more people on.

"I really enjoying spending time with you," Austin said softly. "More so than other people."

"I enjoy spending time with you, too," she said, and she meant it. "Thank you for the bear."

His smile grew. The wheel inched upwards, stopping again after a short time. "I know that you want to go to university out of state."

"Well, my parents might not let me go. If they let me apply to university, it'll probably be the one in town."

"At least you'd be close."

She looked out over the crowd, not sure how to reply. She could see people laughing and running around the fairgrounds, moving between exhibits and games. Their lives seemed so much easier than her own.

"I know our parents want us to get married," he continue, "and I'm sorry because I know it's not what you want. And I'm sorry that I like you, because I know it makes things harder, but there aren't a lot of girls in this town that I could see myself being happy with. My parents always say that they married their best friend, and I think that it'd be nice to spend the rest of my life with someone who's a great friend."

Hannah's heart broke a little. "Austin, I really like spending time with you, too. And I wish that I didn't feel so much pressure, because it'd be easier if I could choose my own feelings. But I think it's a nice idea to marry a friend."

The wheel continued, stopping when they were at the top.

"We could give it a try," she said, hoping that the words sounded less robotic than they felt. "See if it works out."

"I'd like that."

"Good," she smiled.

He smiled back at her. "Could I... Could we try a kiss?"

Her eyes widened, but she quickly hid her surprise. This was what normal kids did, kiss on the Ferris wheel. At least they were high enough up that not many people were paying attention to them. As she leaned towards him she wondered if she was doing the right thing, but then she closed her eyes and saw the face of her crush – her wavy brunette hair cascading down her shoulders, her soft lips, her wide smile that lit up her entire face. As Austin's lip met hers, she imagined that it was Gina sitting next to her, wanting to kiss her, to touch her soft skin, to taste her lips.

A familiar feeling rose up inside of her as she thought of Gina, a spark that started to grow into pure electricity. Hannah could feel her arm-hair standing on edge as the kiss deepened, the electricity filling her up. It was nice at first, but suddenly it became too much, building too fast, seeking an escape.

A loud popping sound pulled her from the moment and she broke away from Austin, pressing back into the seat. People on the Ferris wheel screamed as the decorative lights began to shatter around them. There was a screeching metallic sound as the wheel ground to a halt and went dark, the electricity that powered it suddenly gone. Someone started to cry as another person yelled to be let down. On the ground someone called out "It's all right, it'll be okay, we'll get you down. Don't worry."

The Ferris wheel wasn't moving and she was trapped at the top. Hannah looked around frantically, wondering what had happened. Was this because of her? Was her power real? The millions of questions in her brain were sudden replaced by one realization: Austin hadn't said anything.

Looking over at him, she noticed that he had slumped in the seat, his head hanging down. She gently shook his shoulder. "Austin? Austin, are you okay?" He didn't answer. Holding her breath, she moved her hands to his head and lifted it up. When she saw his face, his lips black and charred, his eyes burned out empty sockets, she began to scream.

DRAMATIC FICTION

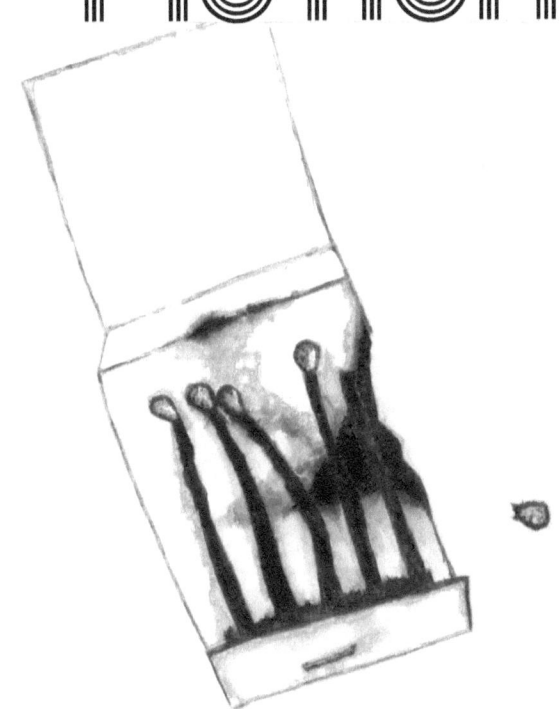

Amphora

They say anything that happens twice is a coincidence, but if it happens three times it's a pattern. Of course, that assumes you're watching out for it. You could have a black cat cross your path every time you walk to work, but if you're distracted and never notice the cat then you won't see the pattern.

I hadn't been paying attention so I didn't catch on until the fifth time.

The first was a train derailment due to bad weather. The second was a swimming incident on holiday, while the third was a trip to the local corner store minutes before a hold-up. The fourth was a car accident, caused by a drunk driver, and the fifth was an airplane crash due to mechanical failure. Each was slightly different in execution, but the result was the same.

When I finally recognized the pattern I was home, watching television footage of the crash. Most stations had switched to the story, pouncing on the unexpected break from normalcy, so it was almost impossible to escape. It had been a while since there'd been an incident like this and reporters were crowded around the outside of the crash site, cameras pointed in, zoom lenses pushed to the limit. As they tried to explain what went wrong, I couldn't help wringing my hands as I watched people stumble away from the smoking hull, towards waiting ambulances. It was difficult to make out features, but I kept watching, hoping that I would see him.

It was possible that he was one of the many injured, but deep down I knew that the worst had happened. I knew this because as I sat there I was reminded of the past and how I'd been through some version of this many times before.

The truth was suddenly both obvious and inescapable. Over the past ten years every person I loved died.

My family and friends seemed to be safe, but I think it's because that's a different kind of affection. The love I'm talking about is the 'want to spend the rest of my life waking up next to you' kind of love. It's a 'want to spend endless hours around you and we don't have to say a word', and a 'want to be with you even when I'm angry at you' kind of love. Whenever I reached that point in a relationship, the invisible clock started ticking down towards an unknown doom. Sometimes we had a year and sometimes it was only a few weeks, but never more than sixteen months.

I'd never had the chance to tell him how I felt before the plane crash. Now I never would.

Once I realized the truth, I vowed to never love again. I stopped dating altogether, and whenever I saw a potential for love, I put a stop to it right away.

On my more cynical days I would try to tell myself that I was lucky. At least I never fell out of love with anyone. I never had to deal with the pain of a significant other cheating on me, or the heartache as a lover slowly slipped away over time, or the devastation of hearing someone I loved tell me that they no longer loved me back. But these thoughts could do nothing to repair the aches in my heart or the torment of having someone taken away from me and trying to live with the hole in my heart where they used to reside. The agony of knowing that loving someone would result in more heartbreak than I'd ever wish to inflict on anyone.

It was my curse, but it was also my responsibility to make sure it never happened again.

But sometimes love can't be stopped. Sometimes it sneaks up on you, and you don't realize that it's there until you're reading a newspaper story about another car accident and you recognize the name, and you hear your heart breaking all over again. Even if I refused to call it love, every touch and smile and laugh betrayed me. We had never actually dated or said the words, but the curse knew what was truly in my heart.

There was only one way to stop it for good.

The knife had been my grandfather's and had been passed down to me by my mother. Looking at it, I remembered how my grandfather had constantly fought with his wife, and how miserable the two of them had been. I remembered how my mother refused to talk about my biological father and how she made so many excuses not to date. Was it possible that this curse was hereditary? If so, would it have been better or worse if they had warned me? I wasn't sure.

The knife had a curved blade and a handle that had once been inlaid with many jewels but now held only a single small ruby. As I turned the knife towards my chest I noticed that it suddenly seemed to weigh less than before. It also felt comfortable in my hand – as if it had been made especially for me.

I pressed the knife to my skin and cut my chest open, reaching inside. Once the deed was done, I laid the knife aside and looked at my heart which I now held in my hand. It was dripping with fresh blood, but I could see the bruises and cracks from so many heartbreaks. Even though it was no longer a part of me, I could still remember the agony that had brought each injury.

Despite the pitiful state of it, I could not bear to throw it away. Instead, I found a clean jar and carefully placed my heart inside. As I closed the lid I felt the empty space within my chest filling with coldness, spreading out to my hands and feet. Placed the jar on my bookshelf, I stared at it. Now that the deed had been completed I wanted to smile in triumph, but my mouth would not obey. Instead I nodded solemnly to myself.

It was done. No more love; no more death. No more.

The Weapon

She awoke to whiteness. As her eyesight came into focus she realized that she was lying on a metal gurney in a room with white walls. Her limbs moved sluggishly as she tried to push herself up into a sitting position and the first few attempts failed. On the fourth, she finally managed to sit up and get a better view of her surroundings – not that it helped much. The room was remarkably nondescript and unfamiliar.

Her skin itched and her head felt as if it had been stuffed with cotton. The last thing she could remember was being in the woods with her unit. They were under heavy fire from the enemy, trying their best to fight back, when suddenly there was an explosion. That was where her memory ended. Had she been injured? This room didn't look like the hospital back at headquarters. And if she was here then where was the rest of her unit?

Trying to ignore the fog in her mind, she looked around for clues, but there was nothing in the room except the gurney and her. There were no windows but there was a door. It took an immense amount of effort to push herself off the gurney and stand on her own two feet, and even though she wavered she felt a sense of triumph in being strong enough to support herself.

As she slowly shuffled towards the door – one foot forward, then another – she wondered if it was okay for her to be moving around. If she had a concussion then she should be lying down and giving her body time to heal. But as logical as that sounded she couldn't rest until she knew where she was.

Finally she reached her destination and grabbed the doorknob. A frustrated groan escaped her lips when she realized that it was locked. All that effort had been for nothing. Looking back at the gurney, she couldn't help seeing it as something sinister and foreboding. Gurneys were for dead bodies, not living, breathing people. What was she doing here? Where was everyone else?

Stepping away from the door, she put her back against the wall and slid down until she was in a sitting position. It was a relief to no longer be standing. After a few minutes her eyelids started to close and her head tipped to the side. It wasn't wise to sleep in an unfamiliar place, but she was having trouble keeping her eyes open. Maybe a few minutes of sleep would help her head stop hurting and bring her strength back. Besides, if she was in a hostile location, they'd already had plenty of chances to kill her. Maybe she was in friendly territory after all.

***

When she awoke, her headache had downgraded to a dull throb and it was easier for her to think. Her skin felt normal, except for a small, itch at the back of her neck. The image of a spider sitting back there, fangs digging into her skin, popped into her mind and she quickly brushed her hand over her neck in the hopes of removing any insects that might be there – imaginary or not.

She was about to stand up when the door opened and a tall man with dark hair entered the room. He was wearing a white lab coat with green scrubs underneath and his shoes were covered with paper slippers. He didn't look familiar.

"Good afternoon," he greeted her, smiling. The smile never reached his eyes and his voice was shaky.

"Where am I?" she asked.

"You are safe," he replied.

"Okay... But where am I?"

He swallowed hard, but didn't say anything else. Before she could repeat her question, he held out his right hand for her to take.

Looking at it warily, she saw that his arm was shaking. Was he afraid of her? Or was he naturally nervous and weak? Did he skip breakfast this morning? It was logical that she was in the enemy's territory, what with the lack of familiar contact, introductions, or even civility, but she didn't understand why she was still alive. Maybe they were keeping her as a prisoner of war, to be traded for the soldiers her own side had locked away.

She could have stood up on her own but this seemed like a time for compliance. It would also be a good idea for them to think she had been weakened and underestimate her strength – something like that might come in handy later on. Taking hold of his hand, she allowed him to help her stand.

Once she was on her feet, he gave her hand one final squeeze before letting go.

"How are you feeling?" he asked, his voice shaking more than before.

"I'm okay," she said, looking at him warily.

His expression was a mix of intensity and fear and she had a feeling that something was wrong. Sure enough the man soon started to waver, balancing unsteadily on his feet before falling towards her. Instinctively, she jumped to the side. Instead of raising his arms to catch himself, he fell into the wall and slumped to the floor. Backing away, horrified, she watched as his body began to convulse, blood spilling from his mouth and eyes and pooling onto the floor. The door burst open and a group of people wearing haz-mat suits raced into the room. Two of them grabbed her arms and hauled her out of the room.

"What's going on? Where are you taking me?" she yelled as she struggled against their grip, but they offered no answers and refused to let her go. They brought her through a maze of corridors to a room full of holding cells. Throwing her into an empty cell, they locked the door behind her and left without a word.

"Who are you?" she demanded, rising to her feet. She pulled on the cell's bars but they wouldn't budge. She had to be in the enemy's camp – her own people wouldn't treat her like this – but what was going on? What had happened to that doctor?

"Ellis...?"

She turned to her left, in the direction of the voice. It sounded tired and old, yet somehow familiar. Drawing closer to the bars that separated her cell from the next, she saw someone moving in the shadows.

"Who's there?" she called out in a low voice.

The person coughed. "Mitchell."

Her eyes widened. Mitchell had been missing for three weeks, ever since he'd gone on a recon mission with his team. Everyone had assumed that the four of them had been captured or killed.

"What happened? Where are Farrow and Smith and Levi?"

He slowly stepped forward. "Gone. All gone. I'm the only one left." As he came further into the light she could see that he was in bad shape. He'd lost a lot of weight and there were dark circles under his eyes, but that was nothing compared to the black blotches on his skin. It looked as if he'd been burned.

"What did they do to you?"

He looked down at the floor. It sounded like he was softly counting to five.

"Mitchell...?"

Looking up, he stepped closer to the bars.

"They started with Farrow," he said, his voice cracking with emotion. "They took her, but we never saw what they did. We only heard the screams. When the screams stopped, they came for Levi, taking him in the middle of the night. A few days later, when he went silent, they came for Smith. I had no idea what they were doing, I only knew that it was terrible. When they came for me..." he paused, counting to five under his breath before continuing. "I'd been expecting torture, like knives and hammers and pliers, but it wasn't like that. This isn't an ordinary prison, Ellis, it's something much worse. They strapped me to a table and injected me with... something. It burned in my veins, made my entire body feel like it was on fire. And then my skin began to burn."

He stepped closer and she could see how the skin on his face and arms was charred and flaking. The bite on the back of her neck started to itch, but she ignored it.

"I'm going to get you out of here and back to the base," she said. "There's got to be someone–"

"No, Ellis. I won't make it."

She grabbed the bars that separated them, wrapping her hands around the cold metal. "I don't want to hear you say that. You can't give up."

"I gave up long ago," he said. He reached out and put

his hands over hers, pausing to count to five again. The skin on both hands was charred and the fingers on his left hand could barely move.

"Mitchell..." She wished that she knew what to say to make him want to fight.

"It's okay. I've wished for death for so long, but they wanted to keep me alive. The treatment didn't work on any of the others. It never really worked on me, but I didn't die, so they kept me around to study, to help make it better. Nobody else came close to surviving like I did. Until you."

Confusion crossed her face. "What do you mean? I wasn't given any treatment..." her voice trailed off as she realized that she had no idea what had been done to her while she was unconscious.

"I know it doesn't look that way, but they must have perfected it somehow."

The back of her neck itched again, and the memory of the doctor flashed in her mind. She remembered how his body had shaken and contorted, how it made impossible angles before going deathly still, and how the blood had pooled under his body, seeping into his white coat. Then she remembered that he'd started to convulse seconds after he'd touched her hand.

"No," she tried to pull her hands away from the bars, but Mitchell had a tight hold on them. After a few pulls, she managed to free herself from his left hand, but his right wouldn't let go.

"They refused to give me the one thing I wanted," he said, tears filling his eyes. "But you can give me this. You can free me."

"Mitchell, please, no, don't. We'll find another way."

"I've already found my way." A large shudder went

through his body and he smiled at her through his tears. "Thank you."

His grip weakened and his hand let go of hers as he fell to the ground. As much as she wanted to close her eyes, she couldn't look away as his body convulsed. Although his face contorted in pain and blood began pouring from his mouth and eyes, she could see peace in his expression.

When he finally went still, she still couldn't take her eyes off of him. Before her capture she'd heard rumours of all the terrible things the enemy had done, but the truth was far worse than she could have imagined. Holding up her hands, she tried to see what they had done to her, how they had made her able to kill with one touch, but nothing looked different. Her skin looked exactly the same.

Her hands clenched into fists as she looked down at Mitchell's body. They would pay for what they'd done – to Mitchell, Farrow, Levi, Smith, and her. She would see to that. She was going to make them suffer – every last one.

Last Crossing of the Night

There were still ten minutes before the last ferry departed. Inside the terminal sat a solitary figure, unperturbed by the dim lights or the uncomfortable plastic chairs. She stared out through the large window at the back, looking at the dark waters that she would soon cross.

Footsteps echoed as someone entered the cavernous room, but she didn't look up or acknowledge the other person. Her eyes remained on the water, a dour expression on her face.

The newcomer looked around the terminal, taking in all the empty chairs. He took note of the clock above the terminal doors and the minutes left before the ferry would arrive from the other side of the harbour, let off its passengers, and prepare for the final crossing. He walked to a seat a few chairs away from the woman, taking note of her expression as he sat down.

"Nice night, eh?" he said aloud.

The woman was startled by his words, but she quickly regained her composure. Looking over at the man she saw that he was at least twenty years her senior. He was dressed in casual, workman's clothes that had seen better days, but his smile was friendly and not alarming.

She nodded politely before turning back to the water.

"Yessir," he said to himself. "Nice night."

The two of them sat quietly for a moment.

"Good thing I made it in time," the man said. "The wife'll have my head if I don't show up 'til tomorrow morning. She knows what happens when I says I'm going out for one drink, but at least I comes back before the morning. I'll owe her some money when I gets home. She always bets me that I'll be gone for at least two drinks, and she always wins. Some days I think about coming home after one, but I'm pretty sure she'd die of shock." He laughed to himself. "Sorry for talking so much, but I'm not good with silence. Even when I'm out on the boat with the b'ys I can't stop jabbering. They likes to say I'm the worst fisherman to ever set foot on a boat 'cause I can't shut up and I scares away all the fish."

"I thought fish didn't have ears," she couldn't help remarking.

"That's technically true, but don't try to argue that with an old fisherman. Most of them got old superstitions about the waters and you're better off moving a mountain than trying to change their minds."

"Except for you?"

He smiled and nodded. "I keeps up with the times. Just because I'm working an old job doesn't mean I don't stay informed. How about you? What do you do?"

She looked down at the floor. "I don't really do anything anymore."

He took another look at her. "I'd wager to say that you've got a sad story hiding inside you. Now I'm not one to go bothering others when they don't want to be bothered, but I knows a lot of people'd love to have an ear to bend – especially when it's the ear of someone they'll probably never see again."

She didn't respond, but he'd said his peace so he sat quietly and stared out at the water.

"I've been a hand model for ten years," she said quietly. She lifted up her left hand and looked at it, taking in the flawless skin and long, slender fingers. "My mother got me into the business when I was seventeen, and since then I've done nothing else. Maintaining my hand has been my top priority. My mother told me that the slightest scar or blemish would end my career, so I couldn't to do anything that might injure it. I didn't play sports or run, or even do yoga. Everything became a threat, even cooking or holding a glass. For the past ten years I've been consumed by fear. But then, one day, I suddenly realized that I couldn't take it anymore. This was no way to live." She lowered her hand. "I don't know why I'm telling you this, but I came here with the hope that I would be the only person on the ferry. When we reached the halfway mark, I planned on leaping over the side and disappearing beneath the waves."

She stopped talking and looked out at the water.

"A life spent in fear doesn't sound like much of a life," the man said thoughtfully. "Although, and I might be a bit naive here, but I'd hope that there's an easier solution to solving your problem other than killing yourself."

A sad look crossed her face. "I don't know if there is."

"Well, don't let me presume to know how you should best deal with your demons, but I'd bet you a million dollars that there's at least one person out in the world who'd rather have ya living and breathing. Besides, I've been in waters like these many a times – never by choice – and I'll tell you that it's mighty cold in there. Not a good way to go, if you ask me."

She turned to him. "Is it very cold? The water?"

"Bone chilling. You'd probably die of hypothermia before you could drown."

She considered his words and took a deep breath. "But if I still wanted to do this, would you stop me?"

He paused. "Well, I couldn't stop you from going over the edge if that's what you wanted, but I can't say that I wouldn't jump in after you. Wasn't raised to go leaving people behind, especially in dark waters."

"And what if I left and came back another night? When there was nobody else here?"

He shrugged. "I'd feel better knowing that you at least tried something else before giving up entirely, but, like I said, I don't know what kind of battle you're fighting."

She fell silent again. Her gaze fell down to her hand.

Footsteps alerted them to another person entering the terminal, but neither paid the newcomer any attention.

Realizing that tonight was not going as planned, the woman sighed and stood up. "Perhaps I'll sleep on it."

He nodded and gave her one last smile before she turned and walked away.

The fisherman hoped that he had given her some things to consider. He wondered if he'd ever see her again or if he'd end up reading about her in the papers.

In the distance he could make out the ferry coming towards the terminal. He looked over at the clock and saw that there was still five minutes left before the last crossing of the night. His gaze fell on the newcomer, sitting across the room, head in his hands.

There was a gym bag on the seat next to the young man, red with a Team Canada Olympic Logo on it. Taking a closer look at the newcomer, the old man realized that he'd seen him before. He had been part of Canada's Olympic gymnastics team. The young man had been a shoe-in for the gold, but then he'd lost his grip while on the rings and fallen, destroying his hopes of any medal.

The fisherman couldn't help noticing the despair in the young man's posture.

"Nice night, eh?" he said aloud.

The young man didn't look up.

The fisherman nodded to himself. "Good thing I made it in time. The wife'll have my head if I don't show up until tomorrow morning..."

Sacrifice

As the water rose around her, she looked up at the night sky, watching the twinkling stars.

She had witnessed only one ritual in her life, during a devastating drought eleven years ago. The crops had withered, every well dried up; the village was desperate. She remembered how the young woman looked, her blue dress blowing in the dusty breeze, a crown of wheat atop her head. Silent tears fell as she walked into the meadow, towards the newly dug hole in the centre, but she did not cry out for mercy until she was being lowered inside. It was too deep to climb out, and only her cries escaped. The elders recited the rain gods' prayers, speaking loudly to try and drown out the young woman, but it was only after the hole had been filled that there was silence from within. The elders finished their prayers and everyone went home. Six days later it rained.

She knew that everyone was watching her, waiting for her to cry out or try to escape, but she felt unequivocally calm. Being chosen as a sacrifice was an honor, and the crown of flowers weighed heavier than any other crown she could imagine. As the water rose, she remained silent and stoic. Her sacrifice would bring balance to the land and stop the destructive flooding that threatened the village, protecting those she cared about.

Cool water covered her face; she disappeared underneath without a word.

The next day the floodwaters receded.

SCIENCE
FICTION

Second Life

As I sat in the cafe, my hands wrapped around a warm mug of tea, I wondered what the last three years of my life had been like. Well, not the last three years of *my* life, which I had obviously lived, but the last three years of my *other* life.

I should explain…

It started five years ago. I was twenty-five and feeling unsatisfied with my life – not that there was anything particularly bad about it. I had a full time job which paid me a decent amount of money. I had a few friends that I sometimes went out with on the weekends. I wasn't in a relationship, but I didn't mind too much.

My problem was that I didn't know if I was on the right path. After graduating high school I'd wanted to attend an arts college but my parents insisted that I study robotics instead. I did as they wished, and when I graduated I found a job at NovaRobotics, the largest producer of robotic devices in Atlantic Canada. At first I started out on the build line, but after a year I was moved up to quality control. It was a better job, and testing the product was much more fun than building it. The job provided for me but it left little time for my art.

I dreamed of leaving everything behind to become a painter, but I knew that it wouldn't be that simple. I would have to improve my technique, which would involve studying and practice. Classes would require money, and I'd still have to pay for rent and other essentials. What would I do if my savings ran out? And what if I was never 'discovered'? What if I painted and painted and nothing came from it except bitterness and regret?

The truth is that I was too afraid to take that risk.

Some days I dreamed of creating a robot that looked exactly like me, so that it could go to work while I was free to paint. I'd have the best of both worlds. I'd never be able to do it, though, not with Bill 176 making it illegal for a robot to look completely human. But then I found another way...

While on my lunch break one day I was flipping through *The Medium*, a national painting magazine. Inside was an article about a performance artist in Halifax who had decided to clone herself. She'd wanted to work on bigger and more complicated projects, but didn't trust strangers to understand her concepts. The article went on to talk about how everyone had reacted to her decision, but I was more interested in the company that had cloned her – Gemini Incorporated.

Halifax used to have three cloning companies in the city, but now only Gemini Incorporated remained. There had been a big boom in clone production twelve years ago, but it had since trickled off. Most of the cloning done was harmless, with the majority of people making clones of lost loved ones, but then there was a horrible scandal with a rich man purchasing younger clones of himself so that he could harvest their organs. It almost led to the government banning cloning outright, but instead they made the screening process more intricate and created harsher punishments for clone abuse.

I thought about what it would be like if I cloned myself. I would be able to keep my job and be an artist. Yes, there would be two mouths to feed, but I could afford that for a while. Maybe my clone and I would be able to switch places – painting one day and working at NovaRobotics the next.

For days I toyed with the idea. How would I explain to my friends that there were now two of me? What if my clone only wanted to paint and refused to go to work? Would I be able to literally live with myself?

In the end I decided that I needed to explore this option further, so I called Gemini Incorporated and made an appointment.

∞

When I arrived at the company for my consultation I felt a wave of anxiety wash over me. I expected the company to take their consultations seriously, but how serious would it be? Would it be a frank chat or something more like an interrogation? Would they take me to a room with a bare lightbulb and grill me to make sure that I wasn't some kind of organ-harvesting monster?

Or would they think that my reason for wanting a clone was laughable and narcissistic?

The man at the front desk seemed nice enough, smiling as he told me to take a chair. As I waited I tried to calm myself. I had dressed carefully that morning, making sure that I looked like a respectable young adult. All I had to do was try not to sound like a psycho.

After a few minutes the man at the desk let me know that the consultant was ready. He led me down a short hallway to an office that was plain, but nice. The colour scheme of the room was ivory and light brown, which had a much needed calming effect. The woman sitting behind the desk gave me a friendly smile as I sat down across from her. There was no lie-detector or torture device in sight.

She asked a lot of good questions about why I was considering this, and listened intently as I spoke. My reasons must have been sufficient, because after talking for about twenty minutes she said that if I wanted to continue with the process she could schedule me for another meeting in three days' time. There were some things that needed to be looked at before they could officially okay me for the procedure, like my credit rating and background check, but I had passed the first test.

When I came back for my second meeting, I learned more about the procedure and what would be required of me. Once the clone had been aged, I would need to have my memories copied and transferred to her, so that she wasn't a blank slate. They would do this at the last possible minute, in order to give her the most up-to-date information. While they were transferring my memories to her, I would go to one of their rooms and wait for them to bring her in to meet me.

We decided that my clone would be called Rin, since it had been a childhood nickname of mine. I would explain Rin's sudden appearance by saying that she was my estranged sister, whom I was back in touch with, and who was staying with me for a while. It helped that I wasn't from Halifax and nobody knew my family directly.

Gemini Incorporated would provide Rin with identification and other important paperwork so that she would be able to work and travel. The consultant explained that we would be as close as identical twins, except that we would have lived the exact same life and had the same thoughts. From the time we met, it would be important that we try to live our own unique lives. Eventually we would grow into different people, but in the beginning it could be difficult to adjust.

This meeting went on longer than the first, but we covered a lot of information and by the end of it I had a greater understanding of the reality of the situation. At the end she asked if I wanted to take some time to think about it or if I wanted to continue.

I went over all the information in my head. I'd never been one of those people who take crazy chances, but this felt right. So I said yes. I signed the paperwork and they took a sample from me right then and there. They said that it would take two weeks for the procedure to finish, after which I would come in for the memory transfer.

After handing over a sizable amount of money, I left Gemini Incorporated and headed for home. I felt some trepidation about what I had just done, but my excitement quickly took over. Besides, it was too late to turn back.

∞

If you want to know the truth, yes, I freaked out quite a few times during those two weeks. I freaked out big time. Had I made the right decision? Why had I gone ahead with it so quickly? Why hadn't I waited a few days or weeks, just to make sure I fully understood what I'd signed up for?

I was quick about calming myself down, but there was always a new thought just waiting for an opportunity to pounce.

What if she hated me?

What if I hated her?

What would it say about me if I hated myself?

Even as I was walking to Gemini Incorporated to meet

my clone I was trying to calm myself down. Most people would accept that they had already gone this far so there was nothing they could do about it, but I couldn't stop thinking about all the terrible things that could happen, no matter how far-fetched. What if my clone tried to kill me? I didn't think that I had the capacity to murder someone, but if I was thinking it then my clone could think it, and maybe I should stop thinking right now.

To be honest, it was scary to think that someone else was going to have my thoughts in their head. I tried to remind myself that this was something I wanted, that it was a way to achieve a goal I'd had for a long time.

'I can do this,' I thought to myself, over and over – drilling the idea into my head. 'I can do this. I can meet my clone.'

∞

It was oddly strange to stand face to face with myself – almost like an out-of-body experience. Immediately I started judging myself. Was my face really that oval? Why was I walking like that – that uncertain, shuffling gait? Did I think my hair looked good pulled back that severely? Looking in the mirror was one thing, but looking at a 3D representation of myself was completely different.

She looked as nervous as I felt.

"So," she said. "Hi."

"Hi."

There was an awkward moment, but then she laughed. It was the same soft chuckle that I had.

"So, what do we do now?" she asked.

"I guess we go home. Don't worry, it's not far."

She gave me a half-smile. "I know."

∞

At first it was weird being around someone who knew everything about me and my life. When I'd ask her if she wanted something to drink, she would fill up the kettle with water and go straight for the cupboard with the mugs in it. I could only stare as she sifted through the teabags for the cherry blossom green tea – the exact tea I had been in the mood for.

I'd like to say that it got better quickly, but it took a while to adjust to having a clone around. In the beginning we'd go for the exact same thing, like wanting to wear the same shirt or dress, or wanting to read the same book, or eat the same things. Okay, maybe that last one wasn't that bad since it simplified meal times, but the rest of it involved a lot of compromising.

When we went outside people stared at us. We tried to look as different as possible, styling our hair different ways and wearing outfits that weren't similar, but it was unmistakable that we were related.

At first we took turns working and painting, since we both felt the way I had. It seemed like a fair compromise, but problems started to creep up. In order for the swapping to work, the person who went to the day job had to tell the other everything that had happened, down the most minuscule detail. The other person needed to know exactly what work had been done and what conversations had taken place with which co-workers. Some days we weren't sure whose turn it was to go to work because it felt as if we were living the same life.

Eventually we realized that it would be easier for one of us to stay with NovaRobotics and the other to paint full time. But how were we going to decide who did what? Rock/Paper/Scissors was definitely out of the question. I wanted to argue that it had been my decision to go to

Gemini Incorporated and that the whole reason Rin was here was because I wanted to do something different, but Rin had my memories so we both felt the same. She wanted to paint as much as I did, and it would be completely selfish of me to tell her no. Besides, I was beginning to suspect that Rin had forgotten that she was the clone and I didn't want to upset her.

In the end we each flipped a coin. If it came up with one heads and one tails we would flip again until they both matched. It was nerve-wracking. My entire future suddenly depended on pocket change.

The outcome was that Rin would be the artist and I would stay with NovaRobotics. I was sad that I wouldn't be taking any crazy chances, but there was a part of me that was happy I could take the easy route.

After that, things started to go more smoothly. We operated on different schedules so we didn't have to fight over everything, outfits were compromised, and chores were shared. After two weeks it felt like I had a very close twin sister instead of a clone.

The only problem was the issue of space. My apartment was really nice – for one person. With two people living there it had started to feel crowded. It didn't help that Rin was using the place as a studio, since renting an actual studio would cost too much money. She was staying in the guest bedroom, but it wasn't big enough for her to live and paint. It was barely big enough for the bed. Most of her art supplies gravitated out into the living room, taking up space that I wanted to relax in after a long day at work.

Was I seriously considering kicking my clone out?

Before I could broach the subject, Rin saved me. Just like me, she could tell that our living arrangement wasn't

working and that something had to change. So after work
one day she sat me down and told me that she was moving out.

"Where are you going?" I asked.

"Well, I thought about all of my options, and I weighed
all the pros and cons. Staying here might be awkward,
what with there being two of us. Halifax is familiar, yes,
but I think I have to step away from that. Otherwise, what
was the point of all *this*?"

I completely understood.

"So I'm going to move to London."

"...Ontario...?" I said slowly.

She laughed. "England. It's full of great art, museums,
schools, history. I've always wanted to live in England."

"I know."

"My only problem is -"

"Money," we said at the same time.

I knew that this would come up and I was prepared
for it. It would have been heartless of me to create a clone
and then toss her out in the street to fend for herself. I had
yet to recover from the dent in my bank account that the
purchase of my clone had created, but if I tightened my
belt I could help her out. It would be worth it if it meant
that we would both be happy.

"I'll help you with the start up," I said, "but London's
expensive to live in."

"I'll get a job as soon as I can," Rin replied. "And if I
have to get a roommate I'll deal with it. I think it'll be a
great experience."

I pushed my jealousy deep down and put on a smile.
"Then I guess you're moving to London."

∞

It took us a month to get Rin ready to move. Packing wasn't a problem because she didn't have much to take with her. There were a few things that held some sentimental value that I agreed to let her take, but we knew that it would be impossible for her to take anything large. In London she would have to start over from scratch.

The day I took her to the airport, I could barely contain my jealousy. *I* had wanted to move to England, *I* had wanted to be an artist in London, and *I* had wanted to work a mundane job in some coffee shop or bookstore. This should be me, not her. Was the flip of a coin enough for me to give up my dreams?

Rin smiled at me before she went into security. I forced myself to smile back.

"I'm sorry it's not you," she said.

I shrugged. *"C'est la vie."*

"If I crash and burn, can I come back?"

My real smile broke through. "You won't."

"But if I do?"

"Of course. You're always welcome here."

We hugged. Then she walked into security, towards her new life in London.

∞

For the first two weeks we emailed each other every couple of days. Rin would tell me how things were going in London, and I let her know what was happening in Halifax. Her emails were much more interesting than mine, but that was to be expected. There were some interesting things happening in Halifax, so I talked about that – what was closing down, what was opening, what had moved and where. I made sure to email her even if I didn't have much to say.

She had trouble finding a job at first. Our job experience was the same, and there was only one employer on our list – NovaRobotics. We didn't even know how to use a cash register. Rin didn't want to work for another robotics corporation, so she had to search for entry-level jobs.

For the first couple of months she bounced from job to job, constantly trying to find something more interesting and more suitable, gaining skills along the way. She found a roommate and a flat to live in that was small but still within the city. Eventually she settled in a job working at a used bookstore, which enabled her to pay her bills and buy some art supplies. The store was big, so there were other employees for her to talk with, and they carried a lot of strange books. Lots of the books were old, with cracked spines and notes scribbled in the corners. She was able to read during down time and would frequently recommend titles to me. For a while we had our own private book club.

After a while, I received a promotion at work and was moved to a more challenging position. I was still in the testing department, but now I was on the programming side. The group I worked with would test new prototypes before they were released for mass production, which was exciting. It came with a raise and a steep learning curve. I was spending more time at work, so I didn't have as much time to email Rin. Our correspondence slowed down.

∞

After eight months, Rin had settled nicely in London and I'd adjusted to my new job. I'd just finished work on a new seeing-eye robot and hadn't yet started another project, so I made plans to go and visit her. I'd always wanted to see London and now I knew someone who lived there.

When she met me at the airport, it was like we hadn't been apart. We were even dressed similar, in jeans and a green top – green being our favourite colour. My clothing was less worn than hers, and I suspected that she'd bought hers at a second-hand store.

Her apartment was small, but her roommate was nice. They'd managed to decorate the place so that it had a quirky and comfortable feel about it, hanging some of Rin's artwork on the walls, which I looked at with minor jealousy. They had no guest room, but the sofa was comfortable enough.

Rin had made quite a few friends in London, but I never felt out of place with them. If Rin liked them then I knew that I would like them. She had told her friends that she had a twin, so we didn't have to deal with anyone suspecting that one of us was a clone.

She showed me around London, taking me to tourist sites as well as places that most tourists never hear about. We ate at pubs, local restaurants, and I splurged on a few dinners, taking her out to places that everyone raved about.

When my trip was finally over, I told Rin that if she ever wanted to come back to Halifax for a visit that I'd take care of it. I knew that she wasn't earning very much money, and I hoped that she wouldn't be too proud to accept my offer. She promised that she would visit soon, and then I left.

∞

It was five months before we saw each other again. Rin changed jobs again, and was now working at a restaurant in downtown London. The tips meant that she could buy more art supplies and take some classes. My job was keeping me busy, so I didn't have time to think about my own art. The strange thing was that I didn't care as much as I thought I would. Knowing that Rin was out there doing what I couldn't made it easier for me to let it go.

When she finally came to visit me I began to notice the differences. We still dressed similar, but she was taking on a more bohemian style while I dressed functionally. She wore more jewelry than I did, and definitely looked the part of an artist.

Rin was glad to be back home, but she was also excited about what was happening in London. She had reached out to a few small museums and one of them had gotten back to her. They were going to show some of her pieces in their upcoming exhibit and were interested in working with her on future endeavors.

I was insanely jealous, of course.

My work was going well and I liked my new job much better than my last one, but it wasn't as exciting as what Rin was doing. I wished that I had something to tell her, some kind of amazingly interesting thing that had happened, but there was nothing.

The only relief I had was when Rin told me that her life wasn't always easy. I know that makes me sound awful, but I needed something to make me feel like it was okay that I was still in Halifax. Her roommate had moved out and the person she found to replace her had been terrible at paying rent on time. Luckily she got rid of that one and found someone else, but the new person still wasn't as nice as her first roommate. Rin missed living alone, but she couldn't afford it.

The restaurant had cut back on her hours, so she had to get a second job. After weeks of searching she found one in another bookstore. Even though she knew that she could come to me for money if she was desperate, she had wanted to do this on her own. Again, I didn't envy her. I hated the thought of passing out resumes and going to interviews.

At least we still got along. We ate out at new restaurants, had drinks at familiar bars, and visited a few tourist sites we'd never thought to visit before. It was getting more comfortable for us to hang out together. We were no longer an original and a clone, we were family.

∞

But time passed, as it does. I became busy at work and Rin was busy with her art. We emailed each other every now and then, but it was nothing regular. We gradually fell out of touch, as people do.

Rin would update me every so often about what was happening with her. She was still working random odd jobs. Her work was in a few smaller galleries around London and one in Cardiff. She'd sold some pieces, but wasn't able to paint full time.

I was still with NovaRobotics, still working with the product creation team. I'd made the decision to buy a house instead of renting and had been looking around at different properties.

Suddenly we realized that we'd gone almost three years without seeing each other. Our correspondences were short and to the point and had slipped to once every month or two. I hadn't known Rin that long, but I missed her. I emailed her, letting her know that I was planning a trip to London in a month's time. I had another project to finish before I could go, and I wanted to give us enough time to coordinate a plan.

Rin informed me that she was living with a roommate

in a small apartment. There wasn't any room for a guest, so she couldn't offer me a place to stay, but I said that it was no big deal – I could afford to stay at a hotel.

Something about this trip felt strange, but I tried to tell myself that I was only feeling nervous because it had been so long since I'd seen Rin. I honestly thought that I would visit London more, but I'd been so busy with work. Whenever I had time off between projects, I would spend it relaxing or traveling around Canada.

When I arrived in London, there was nobody to meet me. Rin had to work late and couldn't make it to the airport, so I made my way to the hotel and then went for a walk. I felt lonely by myself in such a big city. Perhaps I should have put off my visit until a time when Rin wasn't as busy, but I didn't want more time to pass us by.

∞

So that brings me to the cafe, where I'm sitting with a cup of tea, waiting for my clone to walk through the door and tell me what the past three years have been like.

I was nervous, but I couldn't explain why.

When Rin walked in, I barely recognized her. Her hair was cut short, just to her chin, with blunt bangs. I had always wondered what I'd look like with bangs. She looked glamorous and artsy, with her black clothing and silver jewelry. Next to her I felt conservative and plain in my blue jeans and green shirt.

Rin waved at me before going to the counter to order a drink. When she sat down next to me, she smiled and let out a nervous sigh. It relieved me to know that she was feeling the same.

As she reached for the sugar and milk I wondered when she started drinking coffee. How odd to move to

England and stop drinking tea.

"So, how have things been?" she asked.

"Good. I'm still working at the same place. You?"

"Well, I've been working at the bar for about six months."

"Sounds fun."

"It is most nights. I still have plenty of time to work on my art. I've even started experimenting with clay."

"Clay? That sounds interesting." Actually, it didn't. I'd never had any desire to work with clay.

"Yeah, it lends itself to three dimensions much better than paint. I'm really getting into sculpture – there are so many amazing sculptures around here. Have you been working on any art?"

"Not really. I've been reading a lot, and I've actually started writing. Nothing that's worth being published, but it's something to do." I paused and gave a little chuckle. "It's really funny, actually."

"What is?"

"Well, I bought a house."

Rin's eyes opened wide with shock. "You found a place?"

"Yeah. It's nice and not too small, and not far from where my apartment was."

"That's great! How could you think that was funny?"

"Well the funny part is that I always thought that once I bought a house I'd turn one of the rooms into a painting studio, but instead I've turned it into a library."

Rin looked down at her mug and I wondered if she was thinking about her bachelor apartment and the lack of studio space. I wanted to say something about how someday she'd be a famous artist and she'd be able to afford a better place, but everything I thought of sounded wrong.

"I have some big news too," she said quietly.

"What is it?"

She took in a deep breath and held up her left hand.

My eyes widened as I noticed that one of her silver rings was on her fourth finger. "You're married?" I exclaimed.

"Engaged at the moment, but we'll get married eventually. I was nervous about telling you. I know you haven't been dating much."

"I've been dating," I said defensively. "Last week I went out with an accountant."

"An accountant? That sounds boring."

"He was actually really nice."

"Sorry, I didn't mean it that way."

I took a drink of my tea and told myself not to be so touchy. The problem was that I didn't know what to say. I couldn't believe that Rin was engaged. I knew that she'd been dating someone, but I had no idea it was so serious.

"I want you to meet him tonight, at dinner. I hope you'll take it easy on him."

"Why would you say that?" I asked.

"Well, he's a musician."

I didn't say it, but I was surprised. I'd never had much of an interest in music. "Is he good?"

"Yeah. The band he's with plays a few bars around town. They're really popular in Scotland."

"He must travel a lot."

"A bit, but it gives me some time to myself in our tiny apartment. He's great – you'll see."

I smiled back at her, hoping that I'd like him. In the past if Rin liked someone I'd know that I would too, but at this moment I really wasn't sure.

∞

As my plane flew over the Atlantic Ocean, I reflected on my trip. Derek, Rin's fiancé, was nice enough and they were happy together, but I still couldn't believe that she was getting married. Neither of them had a steady job and both were still hoping for their big break. At least they made each other happy.

Maybe I felt lonely at times, but I was happy to have a steady job and a home of my own. My life was less exciting, but it was comfortable and warm and suited me just fine.

It was strange, but I couldn't think of Rin as a clone anymore. She was a whole other person, completely separate from me. I couldn't help wondering if I would have become like her if I'd moved to London or if would have turned into someone else entirely.

I thought back to the day we first met – how anxious I felt walking down the hallway, standing outside the door to the room she was waiting in, wondering what she would be like. I remembered opening the door and seeing her standing there, looking just as nervous as I felt.

So much had changed since that day. We may have shared a past, but our futures were completely different.

Fortune Favours The Bold

The temperature outside was freezing, but inside the Kaminnyy Klub it was warm and toasty. The fireplaces were blazing, the food from the kitchen was piping hot, and holding a mug of warm cocoa could almost make a person forget about the sub-zero temperature outside.

"You know, if most bosses had a choice, they'd give their crew time off on a warmer planet," Levi remarked, taking a sip of cocoa. He'd unzipped his large, down jacket, but had yet to take it off, despite the woollen sweater he was wearing underneath. His dark green hair was stuck up on one side of his head, but he didn't seem to notice or care. Or maybe he didn't want to risk losing any warmth by taking a hand away from his mug to smooth it down.

Captain Pilar Argus smirked in response, unconsciously smoothing her own silver hair. "You knew what I was like when you agreed to work for me," she replied. Her jacket was hanging on the back of her chair, as she was perfectly content with the amount of warmth coming from the fireplace.

"Well, I have a lot of regrets," he muttered.

She didn't take his remark personally. Argus had grown up with Jonas Levi and worked transport with him for over fifteen years, so she knew how much he hated being cold. Unfortunately, his being her second-in-command plus her oldest childhood friend meant that she got a certain pleasure out of tormenting him.

"You know, you could have stayed on the ship," she said.

He shook his head. "Not until Banu manages to get his super-heater invention up and running. It's much warmer here."

They were on Klatch, the outermost planet in the Rossija system, which meant it was the coldest and least populated. Earlier in the day they'd finished their current job by delivering a shipment of goods to one of the speciality stores a few blocks away. While she could have taken off for a warmer destination, Argus had decided to stay on the planet for a little break. It was partly to torment Levi, and partly because she wanted some different scenery after spending the last five and a half days in hyperspeed, travelling here from the Diota System.

Although Argus wouldn't want to stay too long, she liked how quiet it was. On warmer planets, there were always so many people going around at all hours of the day, and everything was so crowded and loud and annoying. Being on Klatch was like a breath of fresh air. Really cold air, but still fresh.

"Um... I think we have might have a situation..."

Her mug was halfway to her lips when Levi spoke. Sighing, she put the mug down and looked at him. He motioned his head towards the left. Even before she saw it, she knew the problem had something to do with her pilot, Aja Kanto, and the ship's doctor, Vera Quintas. Sure enough, they were part of a group of people who had all risen to their feet and were talking angrily with each other.

"What are those two up to now?" Argus said under her breath. Any time Quintas went out in public there was a chance of a brawl breaking out, but she'd been hoping that this restaurant would be relaxed enough to avoid any misunderstandings. The doctor, despite being in her mid-forties and small in stature, managed to find offence in almost everything, and one night in particular a bar had almost burned down after someone remarked that she'd look good in green. Argus had been hoping that Kanto, despite being only twenty-two, would be able to keep the doctor in check, but apparently that had been asking too much.

As Argus drew closer to the group, she picked up on the conversation, which was a heated discussion about who was the better pilot. And now she knew how Kanto had become involved.

"Any place! Any time!" Kanto yelled at the red-haired woman standing in front of her. The woman was half a foot taller, so she had to stand on her tiptoes to make up some of the difference. Quintas was standing next to Kanto, her arms crossed over her chest, grey eyes narrowed in anger.

"Tomorrow," the woman said. "Solnechnyy Restoran on Istra. First one to arrive wins."

"Bring it!"

"Yeah," Quintas said, jutting out her chin. "Bring it!"

"We'll see who brings it at noon tomorrow," the woman replied, smirking.

Argus quickly placed herself between Kanto and the red-head. "Hold on. What's going on here?"

Kanto paled at the sight of her captain, but Quintas wasn't as worried.

"We're going to kick their butts in a race tomorrow," Quintas said, her voice filled with arrogance.

"Or, we're not," Argus replied pointedly.

The woman laughed. "Should've known you two would have an excuse."

Kanto glared at the woman before putting an arm around her captain's shoulders and leading her away from the crowd. "We have time to fit this in, right?" she asked in a low voice. "You always have a few days buffer between jobs, so we've got time, right?"

"That's not the point," Argus said. "We're a business, not a bunch of bored space-racers."

"But she's *really* annoying," Kanto replied. "I want to wipe that smirk off her face *so* bad. I mean, she didn't believe that we outran pirates in the Daehan System last week, but we did."

Argus held back a sigh. "And racing her to Istra will make her believe that?"

Kanto shrugged. "It's worth a shot."

She looked over at Levi, who was shaking his head. They'd done their fair share of racing in the past, but now they were too old and responsible to get caught up in petty squabbles. It'd be best to put the brakes on this and go back to their drinks.

"Look," Argus said, walking back to the crowd. "Unfortunately, we've got better things to do than race some stranger across the system. So, on behalf of my crew, we're going to have to decline your offer."

"Sorry about that," Levi added, not sounding sorry at all.

The woman smirked. "No apology needed. I knew she'd find some way to weasel out of this." She laughed wickedly. "I mean, look at your ship. There's no way you'd win any kind of race with a lowly EOS-class. It's no wonder they stopped making those piles of junk."

"Excuse me!?" Levi and Kanto shouted in perfect unison.

Argus' violet eyes narrowed. "You'd best choose your next words carefully," she said in a low voice.

The threat did nothing to the woman, who rolled her eyes. "Either your ship can handle a race or it can't. It's not my fault if it or your crew aren't good enough. You know, you should've consulted someone who knew a thing or two about ships before making such a terrible purchase."

Argus stepped forward until she was directly in front of the woman. At six feet tall, Argus was the tallest member of her crew and, unlike Kanto or Quintas, she was able to go eye to eye with the stranger.

"Name and ship."

"Ilia. The Rumble. It's a Zeus-class." She smiled confidently.

Argus knew that those ships had a better speed than hers, but she also knew that her ship had something the Rumble didn't – something that would give them the winning edge. "You've got one chance to take back what you said about my ship and walk away. If you don't, then you'll end up having to eat those words."

Ilia closed her mouth and remained silent.

Argus' eyes narrowed. "I'll see you tomorrow at noon." She turned and walked back to her table, to get her coat. It'd be best to get out of the restaurant before she did something she'd regret.

As she moved to the door, the rest of her crew were quick to catch up with her.

"That was so amazing!" Kanto cheered quietly as they bundled up. "You were so powerful and commanding! You were awesome!"

Argus didn't respond. Truthfully, she hated that she'd let herself be goaded into a race by the other woman. Ilia had played them all like fiddles, knowing exactly what to say to get them riled up, and she hated that it had worked so well. Although she had no doubt that her ship would be able to win this race, she had better things to do than get caught up in petty bets.

When they reached the ship, they were greeted by a wall of heat. It was such a change from the outside temperature that they started peeling off their many layers, lest they sweat to death.

"Banu?" Argus called out to the ship's mechanic, hanging her coat up along the wall.

The door to the galley slid open and a pale face with blond hair and white eyes looked out at the group. "You're back."

Argus nodded.

"There was a bit of a situation," Levi said. "Best for us to leave quickly."

"Nice job getting the heater going," Argus said.

Banu looked down at the floor. "It was more difficult than I thought it would be, but I figured that it was important for us to have a warm place to sleep tonight, and I didn't know how long we wanted to stay here."

"Well, as luck would have it, we'll be travelling to Istra tomorrow," she said. Istra was the closest habitable planet to Rossija's sun, so they'd have no need for heaters out there. "Although 'luck' might not be the best word."

"I think the word you're looking for is 'spite,'" Quintas said helpfully.

Confusion crossed Banu's face. "I thought our next job was in the Walh System."

"This isn't a job," Kanto interjected. "This is all pleasure."

She filled Banu in on what had happened at the

Kaminnyy Klub as they all moved into the galley. It was the communal area of the ship – part kitchen, part dining room, and part living room. Argus and Levi sat down on one of the couches, while Kanto and Banu took the other. Quintas went over to the fridge to get a drink, before sitting down at the table.

"So, tomorrow we're going to race to Istra and teach this Ilia whose ship is the best!" Kanto finished, smiling triumphantly.

Banu frowned. "But you said her ship was a Zeus-class."

"And?"

"And those ships have thirty percent more speed than we have. Considering the distance, it'll take us almost three hours longer to get to Istra."

Kanto laughed. "You're forgetting about CIRCE! With her, we'll be able to jack up our speed and leave them in the dust!" She mimed dusting her hands off before raising them in the air. Quintas laughed under her breath.

Banu looked down at the floor and Argus immediately sensed that something was wrong.

"Banu?" Kanto asked, finally picking up on his lack of enthusiasm. "What's wrong?"

"I… may have…" he took in a deep breath and closed his eyes. "I may have short-circuited CIRCE in my attempts to get the heater up and running."

The words came out in a jumble, but every person in the room heard them. When he finished speaking, it was so silent that you could've heard a pin drop.

"…Oh…" Kanto's eyes went wider than Argus had ever seen. "Oh, no."

"Can't you just fix it?" Quintas scoffed as she took a drink, already shrugging off the revelation.

"If it were that easy, he wouldn't've said anything," Levi threw at her.

Quintas shrugged. "I should have known we'd find some way to mess up a sure thing..." She picked up her drink and left the galley.

As Quintas walked away, Argus tried to remind herself of all the good work she had done, and how many times she'd stitched up her and Levi after some bad run-ins. Honestly, she knew that the doctor was likely putting on airs to hide her disappointment, but it didn't help the situation. Still, as much as Argus wanted to be angry at Quintas, it was her own fault for not diffusing the situation properly.

It would be easy enough to pack up the ship and move on to another system. In the long run, who'd care if they skipped out on a race with a random person in a bar on a planet they rarely visited? The answer was: she would. Her pride would remember.

Most people throughout the five systems knew better than to insult someone else's ship. It was a low blow, and one that Argus would never forgive Ilia for. She'd purchased the Aurora – or Ror, as they affectionately referred to her – when she'd started up her own transport business. After working in transport for almost a decade, she'd finally saved enough money to buy her own ship, and she'd fallen for Ror. Sure, the model was being phased out, and she wasn't as fast as other ships, and her weapons weren't as impressive, but they didn't need any of that for transporting. She loved that the ship was designed to look like the old shuttles that transported people around the universe, and the fact that it was solar-powered was a huge cost-saver. Batteries didn't come cheap these days.

Ror was also the only home she had left. After the

moon she grew up on had been attacked by the Vanguard, the scourge of the universe, and her family and friends killed, Argus had nowhere to turn to but her ship. And she sure as heck wasn't going to let some other pilot insult her.

She'd thought that they would show up tomorrow and blow past Ilia's ship, leaving them so far behind that they'd have to spend hours in space knowing that they'd lost to a "lowly EOS-class." She wanted to teach Ilia that you couldn't judge a ship by its stats, and that if you wanted to goad someone into a fight then you'd better make sure that they have no chance of winning.

But none of that would matter if they couldn't fix CIRCE. She was one of Banu's many inventions, and one of Argus' favourites. She transferred power from one function to another, so if they were being chased by pirates and needed to go faster, they could take power from their weapons. Or if they found themselves in a particularly terrible asteroid field, they could boost their shields. CIRCE's energy transfers could be a real drain on the battery, but she'd gotten them out of so many scrapes that Argus couldn't hold it against her.

"How long do you think…" Argus finally said.

After a few seconds, Banu shrugged. "I'll need to purchase some items when the stores open tomorrow. I don't have all the materials I need here, and I can't really do anything until then…"

Factoring in when the shops opened, Argus calculated that they'd have about two hours to get CIRCE up and running before the race started. Considering Banu's hesitation, she knew that it would take him that long, if not longer. After doing some more mental math, she came out with a rough estimation of how long they could go without help and still manage to win.

"Could it be done in five hours? Maybe five and a half?" she asked.

He shrugged again. "Probably. If there isn't anything too terribly wrong. Now that I know how to build her, it won't be like creating her from scratch."

She nodded. There was still an opportunity to back out, give up, and run away, but on the other hand, there was still a chance that they could win. She looked over at Kanto, who still had hope in her eyes, before turning to Levi. He looked like he was doing mental calculations, his eyes darting back and forth, and his mouth screwed up in a frown. After half a minute, he looked at her and nodded.

"If we don't win, at least we'll be close enough to the sun to refuel," he said.

Argus nodded. "Banu, go make a list. As soon as the shops open tomorrow, you go out and pick up anything you think you might need."

He nodded and headed for the door.

"Kanto, Levi," she continued, "we should spend some time plotting the fastest, cleanest route to Istra. Kanto, can you get the long-range scanner from the cockpit?"

Jumping up from her seat, Kanto nodded and rushed out of the room.

Once it was just her and Levi left in the galley, Argus let out a loud sigh.

"It's gonna hurt if we lose tomorrow," she said quietly.

"Then let's not lose."

She glared at Levi. "Can't you say something useful?"

He paused to think. "Maybe the Vanguard will show

up and we'll have to call the whole thing off."

Slumping onto the couch, Argus let out another sigh. It wasn't a good sign when she found herself secretly hoping for the Vanguard to appear.

***

The sun was high in the sky, but Klatch was just as cold as ever. Earlier in the day, Argus had done some scouting to find out where the Rumble was parked, which wasn't far away, and then figured out the half-way point between the ships. At fifteen minutes to noon, Levi and she bundled up and headed out.

It was her last ditch effort to get out of this whole mess. If Ilia didn't show up, then Argus could say that she'd tried and leave with a clean slate. They hadn't made any specific meet-up plans, but Argus wasn't about to take off on an hours-long race without knowing her opponent was prepared to do the same.

As the time moved closer to noon, she found herself hoping that Ilia wouldn't show. Banu had arrived back at the ship around nine-thirty with a box full of supplies and had been working diligently since then, but CIRCE still wasn't fixed. Although she trusted Banu's technological capabilities, she didn't feel good taking off without being prepared.

Taking in a deep breath, she checked the time. There were still five minutes left, but the second it went past noon, she was out of here. Levi let out a groan and she looked up to see someone walking their way. Swearing under her breath, she tried to push back all of her doubts and project the confidence she didn't feel.

"Didn't expect to see you here," Ilia smirked, her mocking tone evident despite the winter wear covering most of her face.

"Wanted to give you one last chance to back out," Argus fired back.

Ilia laughed. "I hope you're ready to lose."

"I hope you're ready to eat those words."

The two of them turned away and headed back to their ships, Levi following Argus closely. Nobody wanted to be late starting the race because their ship had to wait for them to get on board.

"One minute to takeoff, Cap," Kanto informed Argus. She'd already warmed up the engines and was ready to go.

Argus shrugged out of her jacket and dropped it on the floor. "As soon as it hits noon, you get off this planet as quickly as possible. And let me know if the Rumble tries to skip out early. We don't race cheaters."

"Gotcha!"

Leaning on the control panel, she went over their plan again. They'd completed numerous long-range scans last night, trying to pick up on any asteroid fields or high-gravity areas or anything else that might slow them down. They had a good, clean path to Istra, but it still wouldn't be enough for them to win without help.

Finally, the clock hit noon and it was time. As Kanto guided the ship off the planet, Argus hoped that she wasn't making a mistake.

Once they'd reached space and stabilized, Levi picked up Argus' coat. "I'm going to go check on Banu, see if he needs a hand."

Argus nodded. "I'll call you if I need you. Otherwise, give him all the help he needs – whether he realizes it or not."

"Aye, aye." He walked out of the cockpit.

Argus sat in the co-pilot chair. She knew that Ilia's ship was already gaining on them, but there was still a chance that they could win. Looking up at the clock, she put her own count-down in effect. They had three and a half hours to fix CIRCE before suffering a humiliating loss.

"Kanto…"

"Yeah, Cap?"

"If this plan fails, promise me that you'll fly us straight into the sun."

***

They were more than three hours into the race and it hadn't been the smoothest ride. One of the asteroid fields had ended up being bigger than they'd anticipated, so in order to not lose time, they'd had to go through part of it. Thankfully, their shields were stronger than their speed.

There wasn't much for Argus to do as they flew, other than calculate how far behind they were. Kanto was holding to the plan, flying her best, and Banu and Levi were still trying to get CIRCE up and running. Quintas was staying out of everyone's way, which was greatly appreciated.

Every minute that passed was one minute closer to failing. Ilia was about twenty-five light-minutes ahead, and in less than an hour she'd be on Istra. As much as Argus wanted to go and see what was taking Banu and Levi so long, she knew that they were doing their best. Next time she'd have to let Banu know that a warm ship wasn't as important as a functional one, and never to do anything that might risk their existing equipment. Still, she had to admit that his heater had worked wonders. He'd made the ship feel like it was on Istra instead of Klatch.

As the clock neared the zero-hour, she started fidgeting. Soon they'd reach the point of failure, where they couldn't win no matter how fast they went. Why had she thought that they could do this? As soon as Banu told them about CIRCE, she should have withdrawn and given up. Her stupid pride was going to be the death of her. Instead of taking a break between deliveries, she was wasting time trying to race a faster ship. Maybe it would be best if Kanto flew them into the sun.

Soon, there were only five seconds left before everything they did was for naught. Four. Three. Argus closed her eyes and prayed that CIRCE would be finished soon. Two. One.

It felt like time had slowed down, but the clock and ship kept going. The point of no return had been passed. Argus slumped back in the co-pilot's chair. There was no way they'd catch up now. Heck, the Rumble would have almost three hours to gloat about their win before Ror landed.

"Cap...?" Kanto said quietly.

"Yeah?"

"Did we just lose?"

She sighed. "Yeah."

"So, do we keep going?"

Argus paused. Right now she wasn't sure which would be worse – to keep going or to give up. If they gave up, then Ilia would have the satisfaction in knowing that they were quitters, and if they kept going, the next four hours were going to be painful – filled with dread for what would be awaiting them once they landed. Neither option sounded good.

Although she didn't receive an answer, Kanto kept the ship on course.

The mood in the cockpit shifted drastically to one of

resignation. Usually, Argus enjoyed watching the flight through space. As long as they weren't dodging space junk or other ships, it could be peaceful with darkness all around them. She wished she could pretend this was merely a normal journey and enjoy it.

Suddenly she heard footsteps running towards the room. She turned just in time to see the door slide open and Levi burst in.

"Punch it, Kanto!" he said, smiling despite his heavy breathing. "CIRCE's back!"

The two women stared at Levi.

"Can't you see the clock?" Kanto asked. "We lost."

Levi looked up. They were now eight minutes past their three and a half hour deadline. He shook his head. "We've still got time."

Argus gave him a flat look. "How? Are you going to get out and push?"

"No, I did the math. We've got time."

She was confused. "I did the math, too."

"And how many decimal points did you go back?" He raised an eyebrow.

Something clicked in her brain. "Kanto, punch it!"

Levi laughed as Kanto pushed the ship to the highest speed. "You're good at math, Captain, but not as good as me."

"Shut up, Levi," she shot back, but it was impossible to keep the glee out of her voice. Her heart started to race as she sat up in the chair. "How long until we reach Istra?"

"Approximately 45 minutes at top speed."

"And the Rumble?"

"Approximately 50 minutes." He smiled brightly. "See, we even managed to give you a few to spare."

The rest of the trip went faster than it should have. Quintas and Banu joined them in the cockpit to watch the scanner as they closed the distance on the Rumble. There was one tense moment when they hit a patch of space debris outside of Yasny, but the prospect of winning seemed to have renewed Kanto's vigor and she flew through it with no hesitation.

Forty-two minutes after they'd reached top speed, they caught up to the Rumble. Argus wished that they could fly up next to them and wave as they passed by, but instead she had Kanto keep a good distance while instructing Banu to hide their ship ID. She wanted Ilia to think that they were still behind them, and to not realize that the ship that'd blown past them was the very one she'd mouthed off about.

"The minute we hit the ground, we book it to Solnechnyy Restoran," Argus informed everyone. "We've got a five minute head-start, which isn't much time, and I want us to be laid back and relaxing when Ilia's crew comes in."

"I've reserved the landing spot closest to the restaurant," Levi said. "It'll be faster to walk than to take the ATV, so be ready to go as soon as the ship's parked. Clear?"

Everyone nodded. The competitive spirit had infected the entire crew, including Banu, who hadn't even met Ilia, and they were practically vibrating with excitement.

When the ship touched down, everyone except for Kanto was standing next to the exit. As soon as the engines turned off, the door was open and they were gone. Kanto caught up to them a minute later, having promised Argus that she'd followed proper shut-down protocol and locked the door.

The hostess at Solnechnyy Restoran was startled by

the group's sudden appearance, but found them a table and brought them all drinks. Argus looked around the room, at the unfamiliar restaurant goers, and felt all the tension drain out of her.

Seven minutes later, the door to the restaurant opened and Ilia strolled in with her crew. They were laughing and smiling, but then Ilia saw Argus and her crew, and her expression changed to utter disbelief.

"How did you get here?" Ilia asked as she stormed over to the table.

"I could have sworn that we told you about our ship," Argus replied.

Ilia shook her head. "No. You cheated somehow. You were way behind us."

"Guess our ship's better than yours," Kanto gloated.

"But I've got a Zeus-class!"

"Maybe next time you shouldn't judge a ship by its class," Argus said helpfully.

Ilia opened her mouth to say something, but then she let out a frustrated sound and stomped away.

Argus laughed and raised her glass for a toast.

Twenty-One

"Wake up! It's almost midnight!"

Naydir reluctantly opened his eyes. It was too dark to see anything so he shut them again. He had been deep asleep, dreaming of a beach – not the grainy beach they used to visit in Cambria, but a strange soft white sanded beach, with green water and blue sky going on forever and ever. If he went back to sleep, maybe he could find the dream again...

"Stay awake!" His sister shook him roughly, refusing to let him fall asleep again.

"I'm up." He yawned and pulled himself into a sitting position. He only had himself to blame for this rude awakening. After all, it had been his decision to get a few hours of sleep instead of staying up all night, as his sister had done. It was his personal opinion that she was making a big deal out of nothing, but that was kind of her style.

Moonlight streamed in through the window of their dorm room, and when his eyes adjusted to the darkness he was able to see the determination on his sister's face. She'd been waiting for this day for a long time, and she wasn't going to let a pathetic bodily need like sleep ruin it.

As they waited for midnight, they sat side by side on the floor of their room, backs resting against Zenyth's bed. The other trainees in the Peacekeeper Academy were asleep, so it was oddly quiet. Normally there would be people running to and from training or practicing in the hallways. Even during final exams, the building was never this silent or still.

Naydir yawned and his sister elbowed him sharply. He gave her an exhausted look, but she didn't apologize. They stared silently at the glowing numerals of the wall clock. Finally the time moved from 11:59pm to 12:00am. Zenyth took in a deep breath and let it out slowly.

"So, anything happening?" he asked.

Her eyes widened. "I think I finally understand advanced biometrics!"

"Be serious, Z."

"I got nothing. You?"

"Nothing."

They sat silently for another minute. It was now 12:01am on January 17, 695 years after the Last World War.

Zenyth had been planning this night for the past 16 years and, although she'd accounted for a few different variables, her plan always included something happening exactly at the stroke of midnight.

"I told you that it wouldn't happen right away," he couldn't help saying as he stifled another yawn.

"But it could have."

"Are we really going to sit here and watch the clock all night?"

"Why? We don't have to train tomorrow. We've got a pass."

"I feel stupid."

"It's only been one – I mean, two minutes."

"We can't stay awake for twenty-four hours, Z."

"But what if it happens while we're asleep?" she protested. "What if we sleep through it? We might not get another chance!"

He yawned. "If it happens while we're asleep then we'll probably wake up."

"You don't know that we will."

"You don't know that we won't."

They stared at each other, wondering who would give in first. They both knew that it would probably be Naydir. This wasn't the first time they'd disagreed on something and it wouldn't be the last. One of the worst things about being a twin was that everyone expected the two of you to be exactly the same. Every time the two of them disagreed it was as though they were letting down nature itself.

It didn't help that they looked exactly alike, with the same tall, thin build and round face with sharp features. The only difference was that Naydir was male and Zenyth was female, but even that didn't provide much of a contrast. She would have looked more feminine if she grew out her dark hair instead of wearing it short like her brother, but it was more practical for a peacekeeper to have hair that wouldn't get in the way. Besides, she had no problem with the way she looked, so everyone else could just get over it.

At first glance, it was difficult to figure out who was who, but there was no mistaking Zenyth once she opened her mouth. She was brasher and more opinionated than her brother. Naydir was more diplomatic and practical, and thought about what he was going to say before he said it. They were different, but it was more complimentary than polarizing. Of course they fought, and sometimes they would stay angry at each other for days before finally reconciling or giving in, but they never forgot that they were family.

"Do you think it'll happen at the same time?" Zenyth asked.

He shrugged. "I don't know. I mean, we were born four minutes apart. Maybe it'll happen like that."

"You just want to be first."

"Who wouldn't?" He glanced at the clock, which was now displaying the time as 12:05am. "You know, we weren't born until 10am."

"I'm not going to sleep."

"There's no rule that says–"

"And there's no rule that doesn't."

They stared at each other again. Even with the sparse illumination Naydir could tell that his sister was disappointed in him.

Today was their 21st birthday and it was a very important day. Today they would each receive a vision and make the choice to accept the responsibilities of an element or not. They had no idea when the vision would happen or which one of the six elements it would be – they only knew that it would happen sometime today.

Scientists had been trying to come up with a formula to predict the visions for decades, but tests were still inconclusive. Every time they thought that they had worked it out, they would receive data which did not conform and be sent back to square one. It was as if every Elemental's EDNA was in constant flux until the exact moment of the vision. It was almost as infuriating for them as independent genes.

Naydir had often thought about what it would be like to accept an element. His preference was either earth or electricity. Those elements would be useful, especially when it came to dealing with delinquents. Zenyth, he knew from experience, wanted fire or electricity. He wondered if they would get the same element or different.

There was a chance that they would not have a vision, that they would have no choice and remain neutral, and that chance was why Zenyth refused to go to sleep. She didn't want to be one of the small fraction of Elementals without an element. Nobody knew why some people remained neutral, but scientists were still trying to figure it out – along with all the other anomalies that lay within the Elemental EDNA. It would be disappointing to have no choice, but Naydir knew that there was nothing he could do about it. Besides, he was certain that if they were meant to have a vision then they would have one. He couldn't explain this feeling to his sister. It was just a feeling, and Zenyth didn't care much about feelings.

"Did it happen?" she asked.

Naydir broke out of his thoughts. "What?"

"Did you get it?"

"No."

"Damn. You were spaced out for so long that I thought it happened."

"I was just thinking."

"About what?"

He shrugged.

"Then stop thinking. You're making it difficult for me to tell what's going on."

"I'm not going to talk to you for twenty-four hours straight."

"Twenty-three hours and forty-seven minutes," she corrected.

"Z," he sighed, "I'm going to sleep. I don't want to spend the night sitting here not talking and not thinking."

"No."

"You can't forbid me from going to bed."

"No, but I can be annoying and keep you up all night."

"Zenyth..."

She let out a frustrated growl. "But what if you miss it? It would be horrible for only one of us to get a vision. Besides, I want to share the experience with you, you scorch-mark."

Naydir laughed. His sister could be so sentimental sometimes. "I appreciate the love, but I don't think I'll miss anything if I go to sleep."

"You might."

"And I might not."

Zenyth was silent. He had a feeling that this time his sister would be the one to cave.

"Fine, you can sleep. Just don't go crying to me if you don't get a vision and have to spend the rest of your life watching me do cool stuff while you forever live with your silent regrets."

He smiled and hugged her. "Thank you. I hope you'll take my advice and not stay up all night."

"I guarantee nothing."

He stood up and pulled back the sheets on his bed, ready to go back to that warm, sandy beach. Suddenly his sight went completely black. He saw a vision of the earth cracking open into a giant chasm. Sand and rocks broke apart, falling inward as the chasm grew larger and larger. The vision faded into black and Naydir knew what he had to do.

When he opened his eyes, the room was suddenly bright. He quickly shut his eyes, trying to block out the brightness, but everything was red behind his eyelids.

"What happened?" Zenyth asked eagerly. She'd tried

to get his attention, and when he didn't speak to her, she'd turned on the lights. He had been standing by his bed, motionless for almost a minute. "Did you get one? Did you get a vision?"

He nodded. Now that he had time to adjust to the lights, he could see the joy on his sister's face.

"What was it?"

He pulled up the left leg of his pants. Above his ankle was a dark brown square, about an inch tall.

"Earth?! That's great!" Zenyth hugged him. "Did it hurt?"

"It felt like pins and needles, but not bad."

The Tattoo happened after acceptance and it was a mark that all element-wielding Elementals bore. If someone's claim about an element was tested, they had to be willing to show the mark to prove it. Naydir was really glad that it wasn't anywhere embarrassing.

"I'm not sure how I feel about earth," she remarked, mostly to herself. "It's not as cool as electricity or fire, but it's better than nothing." She sat back down on the floor, across from him. "I wonder when I'm going to get my vision. Maybe four minutes from now?"

"I don't know," he replied. "I guess we'll have to wait and see."

***

Even before he opened his eyes, Naydir could feel the ache in his muscles. He was leaning back against the bed, his legs crossed and head to one side. He couldn't remember falling asleep, but it had been for long enough that there was a serious crick in his neck. He was going to feel sore today.

When he looked across the room he saw his sister sitting across from him, staring at the wall clock with tired, red eyes. The time was 8:27am.

"Have you been up all this time?" he asked, rising stiffly to his feet.

"Maybe."

"...Did it happen?"

She didn't reply.

He wasn't sure what to say. "Well, you probably could have gone to sleep after all."

"Shut up."

Her tone was angry, but he could see the slightest hint of amusement on her face.

"Breakfast?" he asked, stretching out his sore muscles. "I'll watch over you if you space out."

"I suppose."

They changed clothes and headed towards the cafeteria. Breakfast was served until 9am for the recruits, so there was still time for them to eat. They passed by a few other recruits, mostly heading in the opposite direction.

"Happy birthday!"

They turned around and saw Todd jogging up to them. He was shorter and broader than the twins, so the double-hug he gave them was delightfully awkward. Naydir and Zenyth exchanged an amused look over Todd's light blue hair. Their friend would always choose the most awkward option when presented with a choice.

"Thanks," Naydir said. "Are you heading to the cafeteria?"

"Of course – just had to find you two first. So..." Todd continued, his violet eyes sparkling. "Did it happen yet?"

Naydir looked at Zenyth, who was frowning again. He didn't want to leave her out by saying that his vision had come but not hers. She rolled her eyes, giving him permission to speak.

"I had mine last night," Naydir said.

"Congratulations! What Element?"

"Earth."

"Nice." Todd looked at Zenyth. "How about you? Earth, too?"

Zenyth ignored Todd and continued walking.

"She didn't get hers yet," Naydir said quietly.

"Oh... Sorry, I shouldn't have said anything."

"Don't worry about it. I'm sure it'll happen soon. She's just upset because she thought that she'd get hers first."

Todd promised not to mention it again, but as they walked into the cafeteria they realized that Todd wasn't the only problem. As Zenyth walked through the room, people called out to wish her a happy birthday and to inquire about the vision. She was ignoring everyone, but Naydir could practically see the black cloud hanging over her head. He had to get to her quickly and do some damage control.

"I'm guessing someone didn't have a vision yet," a loud voice boomed throughout the cafeteria.

Naydir sighed. It was Iain, Zenyth's arch-enemy. It was weird that Zenyth called him that, but Naydir had to admit that whenever anything went wrong for her, Iain was there.

"The day's still young," Naydir countered. "There's plenty of time."

"Is there?" another voice chimed in. "By my calculations there's less than two-thirds of the day left."

Rinn was Iain's best friend and the two were almost inseparable. Her eyes were a dark brown instead of Iain's orange, but they both had the same light grey hair. Everyone suspected that they dyed their hair so that they'd match, but the two of them insisted that it was natural.

"Just go away," Naydir said firmly. He could see the tension in his sister's body and knew that she could resort to violence at any minute.

Rinn laughed. "Why would I want to go away? Zenyth is so utterly frustrated and..." She paused and a wicked smile crossed her face.

Naydir wished that a piano would fall on her head, or a safe, or a tonne of cabbages, but no such luck.

"Your brother got his vision and you didn't!" Rinn exclaimed. "How amazing!"

Iain burst out laughing. "Congratulations on being a dud!"

Naydir rarely lost his temper, but now was one of those moments when he was ready to beat his sister to the punch. "Leave her alone," he threatened, stepping towards them.

Rinn gave one last laugh and walked away. Iain blew Zenyth a kiss before falling into step beside her.

"Zenyth," Naydir began gently, turning to her, "don't let what they said get to you. I'm sure you'll get your vision soon."

"Don't you have training to go to?" she asked icily.

"I'm exempt. It's our birthday."

"You got your vision, so you can go."

"But didn't you want-"

"I want you to go to training. There's no reason the two of us should miss out." Zenyth stormed out of the cafeteria.

Todd shrugged. "She's got a point."

"Yeah. That's what has me worried."

***

In the end, Naydir went to his classes. He quietly talked to his instructors about Zenyth not getting her vision yet, but the secrecy was pointless. Iain and Rinn were already spreading word about Zenyth's inactivity. Never mind that the day wasn't over yet and anything could happen. When Zenyth got her vision, he knew that she was going to make Iain and Rinn suffer.

At lunch he kept an eye out for his sister, but she never showed. Before he went back to training, he took a quick trip to their room, grabbing some fruit to take to her since he was certain that she wasn't eating. When he opened the door, she was sitting on her bed, staring off into space.

"Nothing yet?"

"Surprise, surprise," she said vacantly. "Maybe I am a dud."

"Don't think that. There's still half a day left."

"You got yours right away."

"That doesn't mean anything, Z. There are a lot of twins who get their visions at different times." He sighed. "Have you eaten anything today?"

She didn't respond.

"I brought you some fruit, but the cafeteria's still open if you want real food."

"Whatever."

***

When training was over, Naydir headed to supper with the rest of his class. He looked around for Zenyth again, but she wasn't there. Instead of sitting down, he left the cafeteria and headed straight to his room.

"This has got to stop," he said as he burst into the room. Zenyth was still on her bed, just like before, and the fruit he'd left untouched. He wouldn't have been surprised if she hadn't moved an inch since he last saw her.

She gave a bitter laugh. "What's got to stop? Nothing's happening – which, I might add, is entirely the problem."

"Snap out of it. You can't lock yourself in a room for the rest of your life."

"It's worked so far. No Iain, no Rinn..."

"There's still time."

"Is there time for you to shut up?" she muttered.

Naydir sat down next to her. "So what if you don't get a vision? Plenty of people don't have elements."

"And most of them are duds or stupid, jerky Humanists."

"I'd rather be a dud than a Humanist. Besides, only jerks refer to vision-less people as duds," he remarked.

"Well, it's an appropriate term, because I feel exactly like a dud right now."

Naydir had no idea what to say to her to make her feel better. "How about I get us some food before supper ends?"

Zenyth muttered something that he wasn't sure he wanted to make out.

When he left the room, he ran into Todd.

"What's going on?" Todd asked, concerned.

"She thinks she's a dud."

"So what if she is? You don't need an element to be a peacekeeper."

"It helps."

"Okay, fine it helps. But you still don't need one. I mean, my birthday's not for two months. What if I turn out to be a dud? It won't be the end of my world."

"Yeah, but you know Zenyth. She's been waiting for this forever."

Todd frowned. "There's still time. She could still get a vision."

Naydir sighed. "I hope so. I don't know what to do if she doesn't."

***

Naydir brought back a tray of food from the cafeteria. He'd finished his supper quickly, but Zenyth's plate remained on her desk, untouched. Currently he was torn between demanding that his sister eat something and offering to eat it for her.

They sat in silence for hours. She refused to talk. He tried reading, but nothing held his attention. Normally he liked a bit of silence, but Zenyth's unmovable attitude was driving him crazy. He'd rather be in the training room, testing his new abilities some more, but he couldn't leave her like this.

"Z," he finally said, "it's 10:14. You've been up for almost 40 hours. Go to bed."

"No."

"If it's meant to be, it will be."

She swore and put her head in her hands. "I don't care if it's meant to be. I don't care if it's fated that I don't get a vision. I want one and I can't understand why it's not happening!"

"It's going to be okay."

"No, it's not!"

He didn't understand why she was reacting this way. "Why does this matter so much to you?" he asked.

She looked up at him. "Because you got a vision! When I pictured this night, I entertained the slim possibility that we might not get a vision, but never in my life did I think that only one of us would get an element! You can't tell me that it wouldn't bother you if I had a vision and you didn't."

"It might not."

"It would! We've shared every major experience – our birthdays, our driver's tests, getting accepted into the police academy. But this – this whole thing about me not getting a vision – that isn't something that I can share with you. You don't know what it's like to have to live the rest of your life as a dud. And I won't know what it's like to have an element."

"So what? It's not like we'll suddenly stop being twins."

"But it might be the beginning of the end. This might be the day where we start drifting away from one another. I mean, we're not exactly identical when it comes to personality. What if this drives a wedge between us?"

He shook his head. "We won't let that happen."

She looked down at her hands. "Maybe it wouldn't happen if it was you without an element, but I might let it. I can admit I'm not a big enough person to not let it get between us."

"Z..."

"There's nothing you can do to help. Just be quiet."

He walked over and sat down next to her. "If I could give you my element, I would."

"I know, and that makes me feel even worse."

He was quiet for a few seconds. "I know that we look identical, but we've always been very different people. I think it's what makes us a great team. This is just one more difference."

"Yeah, well it's one that I didn't sign up for."

"Zenyth–"

"I don't want to talk about this anymore." She turned

away from him. "I'm going to go to bed. Might as well get this stupid day over with."

He wished that there were something he could do for his sister. If he could have shared his element with her or given it up so that they'd both be element-less he would have, but it was impossible.

Naydir walked over to his bed and turned down the sheets. When he looked back at his sister, he saw that she hadn't moved. For a moment he'd thought that she was actually going to sleep, but chances were she'd stay awake until midnight. He wondered if she'd ever sleep again.

"You should go to bed," he said.

No reply.

"Z, you should get some sleep."

When there was still no reply, he walked over to her. She was staring off into space, looking at nothing in particular. Naydir looked at the wall clock; it was10:34pm.

"Zenyth?"

She jumped, as if she'd just woken up. A look of relief crossed her face and a wide smile broke out.

His mouth dropped open. "You got a vision?"

She nodded.

"What element? Earth, like me?"

She shook her head and pulled up the right leg of her pants. On her ankle was a tattoo the same size as her brother's, but hers was of two wavy blue lines.

It was fitting, really. Her element was the opposite of his.

Acceptance

He had always wanted to be a hero. As a child, he couldn't wait for the day that he would be big and strong and powerful. Enemies would tremble in his presence, and those who feared him would speak his name in hushed tones. He would use his power to fight wrong-doers and make all of Segment Delta safe for his friends and family.

Once he had helped defeat the evil Council of Twelve, the people who had been under their control would wake up. They would realize that The Council had deceived them, and that their utopia was merely a dream. Then they would turn to the island of Tecken and see that all the lies The Council had fed to them were untrue. Tecken was an island of harmony and prosperity, while the rest of Segment Delta was filled with hatred and cowardice. They would realize that the Erikson family had been right all along, but they'd been too scared to understand.

The Council of Twelve would be destroyed, the island leaders would bow to the knowledge of the Eriksons, and the entire Segment would finally be at peace.

Ø

Nathan Roane waved his stick wildly through the air, fighting and defeating imaginary enemies one by one. "When I grow up, *I'm* gonna be the best sword fighter in the world!" he declared.

"No way!" A girl with dark blue hair called out. "I'm gonna be the best fighter!"

"Nuh un!" Nathan fired back.

"Uh huh!" she declared. Determination flashed in her grey eyes as she picked up a stick of her own.

He readied himself for an attack. "If you want to be Keiko Erikson's right hand fighter then you're going to have to do it over my dead body!"

"Fine!" She raised her stick high, but before she could attack, their friend called out.

"Nathan! Calypso! The teacher's staring at us! If you two don't stop it, we're going to get in trouble again!"

"We can't stop," Nathan replied, his red eyes as serious as they could get for an eleven year old who was fighting with sticks. "This is for honour."

"Why would you get in trouble, Eston?" Calypso asked, putting one hand on her waist and lowering her stick. "You're not even fighting. You're just standing there, like a blob."

Eston crossed his arms angrily and kicked at a nearby dirt pile. "I *always* get in trouble when you and Nathan do stuff, even when I'm not around. It's not fair and I hate it. And if you two don't stop getting in trouble, I'm gonna find better friends."

Nathan looked across the school yard and saw that their sixth-grade teacher was indeed watching them. As much as he wanted to battle Calypso, he knew that Eston was right. This fight would have to wait for another day.

"Fine," he said, dropping his stick on the ground. He gave Calypso one last glare. "But when we're in the Tecken army and I'm the best fighter ever, don't expect me to take it easy on you."

"I'd like to see you try," she taunted, letting go of her

own stick. Once the weapon was out of her hand, her expression changed from serious to playful. "So, what do we do now? Don't say tag. I'm bored of tag."

Eston thought back to the last time they'd played that game, when Calypso had been so intent on tagging him that she'd accidentally shoved him into a bush, resulting in one of the branches scratching his arm so deeply that he'd almost needed stitches. "Yeah, me too," he echoed. "How about stones?" That was a fun, non-violent game.

Nathan looked over to see if their teacher was still watching them, but she was now talking to another teacher. He hoped they weren't angry that he'd been about to fight Calypso again. Teacher Grayson had explained to the both of them many, many times that this rivalry could wait until they were actually in the Tecken army. They tried to tell her that they had to start training now in order to be the best, but there was no compassion to be had. Nathan hoped that they weren't about to get into trouble.

When he looked back to his friends, he saw that Eston had set up a tower of stones a couple feet away. Calypso was putting the finishing touches on the scoreboard, which she had drawn in the dirt with a stick.

"I call first stone!" Eston yelled.

Nathan wanted to argue, but said nothing. Stones was a game of precision and aim, and the final score shouldn't matter on who went first or last.

The game began and they each took turns throwing stones at the carefully balanced tower. Whenever it was knocked over, Eston made sure to build it up the same way. After they'd each gained a few points, he removed a couple of stones, making the tower shorter and harder to knock over.

Calypso was winning by two points when the bell

rang, signalling the end of free play. They joined the other students at the school door, where the teachers were standing.

"Students," Teacher Grayson began seriously, "I have just been informed by Teacher Mai that our beloved leader, Keiko Erikson, has fallen ill. She has been brought to the hospital, where our doctors will do their very best for her. I ask you all to join in a quick prayer to wish Erikson a speedy recovery."

All of the students bowed their heads as Teacher Grayson recited a prayer for health. After the prayer ended, the students were led inside.

"Do you think she'll be all right?" Nathan quietly asked his friends as they waked to their classroom.

"Of course she will," replied Calypso. "I mean, she outlived both her brothers."

"Yeah, but..." Eston lowered his voice. "That's the point. She's old."

"Titus and Elina were older," she countered.

He shrugged. "Well, if she's in the hospital it must be serious."

"People go to the hospital for lots of stuff, Eston."

Nathan wanted to tell them to stop fighting, but he was too worried. Keiko had never been sick before. Were they being told about it because there was nothing to worry about? Or was there another reason?

He had met Keiko a few times through his mother, who worked as a weapons trainer for the army. The leader had always been very nice and intimidating and powerful, and he had barely been able to speak a word to her. His mother teased him about his shyness whenever Keiko was around, but he didn't want to be shy – he wanted to be the best. Nathan often dreamed of the day when he would join the army and show Keiko how good of a fighter he was and how much he could help their cause, but now he was wondering if he would ever get that chance.

Ø

Keiko Erikson's funeral was three days later. Everyone was stunned by the news, as her passing had been so sudden. The illness had been quick and deadly, and although the doctors tried their best they were unable to save her. Only close family members were able to attend the funeral, but vigils had been planned throughout the island.

Nathan had never lost someone he'd known before, and it felt as though there was an emptiness inside of him that he didn't understand or know how to get rid of. His mother tried to reassure him by telling him that at least Keiko hadn't suffered long, but it was little comfort. He had liked Keiko and didn't understand why she had to die.

The loss hit his mother hard. She had been a good friend of Keiko and cried when the news of her death was first announced. By the day of the funeral she was composed, and Nathan tried his best to follow her example and ignore the empty feeling inside. If she could be strong, so could he.

They were attending a vigil at a nearby park, which was a short walk from their home. The weather was sunny and warm, with the trees full of leaves and the flowers in full bloom, but there was no mistaking the solemn mood that hung over the island. Everyone was dressed in white, to show that they were mourning, and a few people clutched bouquets of blue flowers. When his mother and he arrived at the park, there were at least fifty other people gathered.

He knew that Eston would be somewhere in the crowd with his family, but didn't go looking for him. Instead he stood by his mother, holding her hand.

At nine o'clock in the morning, a representative of the Erikson family began the vigil. Nathan had never been to one before, but he knew that he should stay as still and quiet as possible, and keep his head bowed respectfully. There were readings from the History of the Erikson Family, a summary of all that Keiko had accomplished as leader of the island of Tecken, prayers for her spirit, and thanks for all that she had done. The vigil lasted for thirty minutes, after which the crowd dispersed.

However, the day wasn't over yet. In a few hours, Keiko's son, Magnus Erikson the Second, would officially be appointed the new leader of Tecken. Nathan's mother was important enough to attend the ceremony, and he was lucky enough to attend with her. Even though he was still saddened by the loss of Keiko, he couldn't help also feeling excited. Today he was going to witness history.

Calypso and Eston were extremely jealous, since neither of their parents held jobs within the army. Nathan would get to sit in on the whole ceremony, while they would have to stand outside with the rest of the island, waiting for Magus to make his appearance on the balcony as the Sixth King of Tecken.

If he was lucky, he might even get to meet Magnus. His mother had warned him that the chance was possible but also slim. It was enough of an honour to be able to attend the ceremony, and Magnus wouldn't have time to talk to everyone in attendance. Still, Nathan couldn't help hoping that he would get to shake Magnus' hand and tell him how one day he was going to be the best soldier ever.

As they walked to the ceremony, Nathan tried to project confidence and discipline – good qualities for a soldier. He was wearing a navy shirt and pants, the official colour of Tecken, and although it wasn't the same as his mother's official army uniform, it looked close enough.

They were headed to the Community Building, formerly the Inter-Segment Security Building. It stood in the middle of the island, and at six stories high,was the tallest structure on Tecken. It used to be the workplace for representatives of The Council of Twelve, but had been reclaimed after Tecken declared independence. Now it served as headquarters for the Tecken army and housed the Office of Erikson. The building's presence was a reminder to everyone of how they had once been under the control of The Council, and how they had been liberated. Instead of being used to police citizens, it now stood for freedom and independence.

The ceremony took place in the assembly room. It was the largest room in the building and took up the entire third floor. The walls were hung with portraits of the Erikson family, going from Keiko all the way back to Magnus Erikson the First, the liberator of Tecken. The room had been filled with rows of chairs facing a stage and podium, which had been assembled at the back. The room was crowded with people, all dressed in navy uniforms and talking excitedly.

After a few minutes the crowd was called to order and everyone took their seats. A door near the stage opened and a group of people wearing military uniforms entered and ascended the stage. It was the audience's first glimpse of Magnus, and although Nathan wanted to cheer, he stayed respectfully quiet with the rest of the crowd.

The master of ceremonies began. "We have suffered a great loss this week, but we have not lost hope. Ever since

Magnus Erikson the First realized the inefficiency of The Council of Twelve, we have been the leaders of freedom for this Segment. The other islands remain scared and ignorant, and allow hatred to grow in their own backyards, but we strive to be the best. We serve as a beacon for all other islands, showing them how better life can be when each person is allowed to have a say in how they live. So although we mourn the sudden loss of Keiko Erikson, we have not lost hope. Today we appoint her son, Magnus Erikson the Second, as the new leader of this island. We have no doubt that he will lead his people with fairness and diplomacy, and follow the example set by his great-grandfather and all who followed after. We have no doubt that he will continue to give us hope, as his family has done for generations. So, in front of you all, I now appoint the Sixth King of Tecken, Magnus Erikson the Second."

There was a round of applause and the entire room rose to their feet as Magnus made his way to the centre of the stage. Although he was only twenty years old, he carried himself with confidence and assurance. The applause ended and everyone resumed their seats, eagerly awaiting their leader's first words.

Magnus stood at the podium and looked out at the sea of people, taking in the crowd. Once he was certain that everyone's attention was on him, he spoke. His voice was clear and confident, full of emotion and drive. Nathan sat up straighter in his seat and paid close attention, determined to remember every second.

"I had often dreamed of the day that I would stand before you as your entrusted leader, but I knew that it would come at a cost. My mother was an amazing Queen. She cared about the people of this island and did her best for each and every one who lived here. She was always mindful of their interests and concerns, and did every-thing she could to protect us from the tyranny of The Council of Twelve. Other islands within this Segment are satisfied with turning a blind eye to hatred and bigotry, but we refuse to be ignorant. We see this world for what it really is, and we know that it can be better. Through hard work and determination we have rescued this island and its people from The Council's rule and created a utopia. And while we have many enemies who seek to damage us and destroy our peace, we are not helpless. Our army and our people are strong and willing to do the right thing, and we will protect this island from anyone who seeks to do us harm.

"It was my mother's dream to see the rest of the Seg-ment take control into their own hands, as we have done, and no longer live complacently under the rule of The Council. Although she was unable to see that dream come true, it will not die with her. Just as my great-grandfather sought to do away with hate and injustice, I will do all I can to show the rest of the Segment that freedom is within their grasp. The Council does not listen to their people, but the Eriksons always have and always will. As your leader, I vow to protect this island and its inhabitants, and I will stay strong in my resolve to always do the right thing for my people. So although we mourn a great loss today, we see that the future is still bright. As long as there is an Erikson, there is hope!"

The crowd erupted into cheers, jumping to their feet, and Nathan felt an overwhelming rush of pride wash over him.

Ø

"Nathan, it's time to go home."

At his mother's words, Nathan lowered his practice sword and groaned. He had not yet perfected the sequence from class today and didn't want to leave when he was so close. He considered asking for another half hour, but she had anticipated his request and was already shaking her head.

"Pack it in or I'll use this time to reconsider our agreement," she said.

He sighed and walked over to the weapons shelf to put the sword away. It had taken a lot of negotiating to get her to agree to this. First year soldiers weren't allowed to train at the base after hours, but his mother was important enough that he could break the rules. She wasn't fond of the idea that he was getting extra practice time at the base because of her job, however, and was looking for any reason to take that privilege away.

"I've almost got it," he said, walking over to her. "It's just the ending."

She gave him a half-smile. "Your class only learned the sequence today. You have a week to get there."

"Yeah, but you know that Calypso's going to spend all night working on. And she'll probably have it perfect by tomorrow," he grumbled.

She stifled a laugh. "I know that I shouldn't encourage this rivalry between Calypso and you, but it makes you two work so much harder."

"Really, mom?"

She put her arm around his shoulders. "Let's go home. You still have chores to finish before bed."

Their house was only a few blocks away from the training facility, so they walked. The rain from earlier in the day had stopped, and even though the ground was still wet, the sky was clear. While they walked, Nathan's mother asked him about his day. He had spent years looking forward to his eighteenth year, when he would start mandatory army training, but he hadn't realized just how much work it would involve. Not that he minded hard work – he just wished that certain other people weren't so good.

Today's training drills had been fine, but during hand-to-hand combat training, Calypso managed to land a few solid hits, which bothered him to no end. All he wanted was to be better than her, but she kept matching his skill level.

He decided to keep that incident from his mother, but he couldn't help feeling annoyed just thinking about it. "You know, if you'd started training me earlier, I could be so much better by now."

She sighed. "We've already had this conversation, Nathan. Many times."

"I know, but–"

She held up her pointer finger. "Reason one."

He wanted to roll his eyes but knew better. "You wanted me to have a childhood, not a training regime," he obediently recited.

"Reason two."

"You teach people how to fight all day, so you want to have time that doesn't revolve around students and weapons."

"Reason three."

He sighed. "You're my mother, not my personal instructor."

"And finally…?"

"Finally?" He was confused. There had always been three reasons, not four.

"The final reason is because if I started you early, you'd

be so far ahead of the other students that it wouldn't be fair to any of you. You'd become bored in class and start to slack off, and eventually fall behind. Right now you're learning with the others, so you have the chance to show your drive and determination, and stand out from them. It's a good thing – trust me."

He hated to admit that she had a point. "Fine…" he grumbled.

She let out an exaggerated sigh. "Some children only care about playing games, but you've always wanted to be a soldier for the army. Must be our EDNA…"

"So," he said, attempting to slyly change the subject, "have you heard anything about the covert team?"

Sighing again, she shook her head and gave a little laugh. "You know as much as I do, kid. You'll probably be too young to join up, so don't get your hopes too high. Erikson's only going to choose people who've finished their four years."

Nathan couldn't help frowning. He'd heard that Erikson would be sending people out to the rest of the Segment to do reconnaissance and spread the teachings of his great-grandfather, and that the groups were going to be small. While he didn't know exactly what these people would be doing, he knew that it was important. It would be unlikely that a mere first year trainee – one without an elemental power – would get on the team, but if he somehow managed to make the cut it would be extremely satisfying.

"Did you hear what I said?" his mother scolded. "Right now you need to concentrate on your training. There will be other opportunities. And even if there aren't, there's always the island security team."

"I know, mom," he replied. Although he used to

dream of being on the security team, finding spies and punishing traitors, now he wanted to do more. He didn't just want Tecken to be safe, he wanted the entire Segment and all the islands within have the same freedoms they had. It wasn't fair that he had to wait so long to achieve this. Maybe if he worked hard enough Erikson might take a chance...

"Nathan."

He snapped out of his daydream. "Yeah?" He hoped that she couldn't read his mind, although it seemed that way sometimes. Were his emotions that transparent?

She ruffled his blonde hair – an action that made him feel ten years old. "Training first. Everything else can wait."

"Yes, mom." He wondered if other parents were as realistic as his mother or if she was unique.

Ø

Nathan carefully swung the practice sword around his head, bringing it to rest in front of him. He made a few forward attacks, keeping his lines clean and precise, just as he had been taught.

"What are you doing!?" Eston's panicked voice called out, startling him.

Nathan lowered the sword and turned to his friend. "Practicing, of course. What does it look like I'm doing?"

"No, I mean, what are you doing with a sword? Unless..." He raised his eyebrows expectantly.

Nathan shook his head. "Not yet."

"Okay. Then let's get you out of here before any instructors see you. You know, there are reasons why people aren't allowed to train on their 21st birthday, like injuries and death..."

"It's a practice sword," he argued, swiping the fake blade across his arm. "It doesn't even have sharp edges."

"Hey, I don't make up the rules." Eston took the sword from him, put it away, and practically shoved Nathan out of the weapons room. "You missed a great combat class. Calypso was fighting Scott and he'd actually managed to get the upper hand – I have no idea how, it all happened so fast. So, he had her on the ground and he was twisting her arm, trying to get her to tap out, but then she starts laughing. Like, really loud laughter. It was so weird that Scott got all confused and loosened his grip and then she turned the whole thing around on him."

Nathan couldn't help smiling. "Is she upset even though she won?"

"Of course."

"Then we'll have to give her a ton of grief about it later."

He wished that he had been there to see it. If his elemental vision had arrived in the morning, like he'd wanted it to, then he could have gone to class. Instead he was stuck on a temporary time-out until the vision came, which he hoped was soon. There was nothing worse than spending your entire 21st birthday waiting.

There was no way to tell when the vision would come, but Nathan was annoyed that it was taking so long. Calypso had received her vision four months earlier, late in the morning, and Eston's had come a month ago in the early afternoon. Nathan knew that Calypso would never let him forget that he was the last and the latest of their group to Accept.

"Hey!" Eston poked him in the arm. "Was that it?"

"Not yet," he sighed.

They walked out of the base, towards Eston's home.

"Have you given any thought to which element you'd like to have?" Eston asked. He'd wanted the power of Fire, but had received Ice instead. Although it gave him control of both cold air and cold water, he had to work harder just to be as powerful as those who received Air or Water. Calypso had wanted and received Electricity.

When he was younger, Nathan had been confident that he would get the power of all the elements and become the powerful Six-Elemental. It was only fitting that a hero have every advantage, after all. Once his mother became aware of this, she sat him down and explained that the Six-Elemental was a myth and a person couldn't have more than one elemental power. It had been disappointing to accept the truth, but eventually Nathan returned to his earlier unshakeable self-confidence.

"I've given it a lot of thought, but I can't decide," he said. "All of them would be useful in their own way. Maybe Earth, because we've all got to stand on something. I mean, I'll probably get Water like my mom. My biological father had Water, too, so that doubles the chance."

"Well you've already got your mother's sword fighting skills and red eyes, so why not her element. Although you don't have the same hair colour… Maybe you've got some independent genes rumbling around inside of you."

Nathan shrugged. It wasn't his mother's bright red hair that he wanted – it was the dark, black locks of the Erikson family. There was a short time in his life when imagined that his father was actually an Erikson but couldn't tell anyone for political reasons. Unfortunately the timeline didn't work out. Besides, he had seen the file on his biological father, who had orange eyes and the same blonde hair, and was definitely not a secret Erikson.

While they walked, Eston made it his mission to keep

Nathan distracted by asking as many questions as possible. Some of the questions were really strange, and Nathan had a feeling that his friend was grasping for topics, but he was glad to have the distraction. For a while it was easy to pretend that it was just a normal, ordinary day.

Eston's parents had gone out for the evening, so the two of them made supper and filled the time talking about what jobs they wanted after their fourth year was over. It was likely that they'd both end up on the island security team, but they really wanted to go out and infiltrate the other islands. They'd been ineligible for the previous covert team, but maybe someday Erikson would send out another team that they could join.

After supper Calypso joined them, and Nathan made sure to ask about how combat class had gone. Instead of replying she glared at him, and Eston and he burst out laughing. Once their fun was had, they settled into the living room to watch movies. Eston had a great collection of action movies and it was easy for the three of them to sit back and lose themselves in the excitement.

Nathan was having a great time until he happened to catch a glimpse of the clock to the left of the television.

"No…" His voice was low as he rose to his feet. "Tell me your clock is wrong."

Eston looked away from the television and noticed the time. "I... Um, I didn't think it was, but, um, let me check the other clock." He jumped up and went into the kitchen, while Calypso sat silently.

Nathan was frozen in place. How could it be after midnight? How could his birthday be over? He hadn't received a vision. How could he not receive a vision!? How could he be neutral!?

Eston returned and Nathan could tell by his face that

the clock was correct.

"You know… lots of people don't–"

"I'm not lots of people!" Nathan yelled. "I'm supposed to get an element! That's what's supposed to happen! I'm not supposed to be a dud!"

Eston and Calypso wisely stayed quiet while Nathan began to pace. He'd understood that getting six elements was out of the question, but never in his life had he imagined that he wouldn't get an element at all. How was he supposed to be Erikson's right hand man without an element? How was he supposed to keep the island safe when everyone else was more powerful than him?

"Maybe–" Calypso began gently.

He didn't wait to hear the rest – he raced out of the house and into the night.

Ø

The punch came from the right, and even though Nathan deflected it easily, he barely had time to block the kick that came after it. Nexus had obviously been working on her attacks. Luckily Nathan noticed that she still had some of her old blind spots.

He pretended to fumble and when she came in for an easy hit, he landed a blow to her solar plexus. She backed off, a scowl on her face.

"Hit," Kennedy, their combat trainer called out. "That's one to nothing."

Nathan readied himself. Nexus rushed at him and locked him in a grappling hold. It was a big mistake and Nathan was about to toss her to the ground when a sudden jolt went through him. He let go and backed up.

"What was that?" he demanded.

"What do you mean?" she replied innocently.

"You used your element. You're not supposed to be using your element."

"Oh, sorry about that," she said, not sounding sorry at all. "It's just that they're difficult to get under control when they're new. You know what I mean, right?"

Nathan felt his hands clench into fists.

Kennedy shouted out for them to continue and told Nexus to keep better control of her element.

In the end Nathan won three hits to zero, but his opponent managed to 'accidentally' zap him a second time. If it hadn't been a training class he would have pounded her into the floor.

During the fight's post-mortem, Kennedy scolded Nexus for not keeping control of herself and informed her that she couldn't rely on her element all the time – she needed to be confident enough in her own abilities. Then Kennedy pointed out their mistakes and accomplishments, and gave them a list of things to work on.

Even though he had won the fight, Nathan feel terrible. As two new opponents stepped into the middle of the room and prepared to fight, he leaned against the wall, stewing in his own thoughts.

"Don't let her get to you," Eston said, going over to him at the end of the class. "Nexus knew she'd never be able to defeat you in a fair fight. It's kind of a compliment."

Nathan ignored him and stormed out of the room. He was frustrated enough to punch the wall. It was never going to be a fair fight when Elementals were concerned, so why should he take their advantage as a compliment? Before his birthday he'd been top of the class, and now he was nothing but a joke.

"Hey jerk!" Calypso called out.

He didn't stop walking, but he slowed down. "What do you want?"

She jogged up to him. "I want you to know that Eston's still standing where you left him. He looks like a wounded animal."

"So?"

"So, if you keep treating him like crap then eventually you two won't be friends anymore. I mean it's not his fault that you're neutral."

"I know, I just..." Nathan let out a frustrated sigh. "Every time I see his hand, I see his Tattoo, and I just..."

Calypso crossed her arms over her chest. "You remember that we don't get to choose where the Tattoo shows up, right? Just like we don't get to decide which element we get, or if we even get one. All of that stuff is out of our control."

Of course he knew that, but it didn't make it easier to accept. He leaned back against the wall, wishing that he could go back in time, to before his 21st birthday, when he still had hope.

Calypso could see that her words weren't having the intended effect. "I'm just saying that Eston's not like me – if he thinks he's hurting you by being around, then eventually he'll stop being around you."

"Well, maybe that's what I need right now," he replied petulantly.

She shrugged. "Whatever makes you happy. I just know that someday, when you're ready to be friends again, he might not be there. And I can't be sure that I'll be there, either."

As she walked away, Nathan reflected on her words. He knew that she was right and he was putting a long-time friendship in danger, but he couldn't help feeling this way. It wasn't possible to simply bottle his emotions and pretend that everything was fine. What he needed right now was to feel angry, and he couldn't do that if everyone was constantly checking on him and trying to cheer him up.

Ø

Two weeks later Nathan was spending the evening in the training room, letting out his frustration on a punching bag. At every hit the bag bounced around on its chains, trying to swing free from its restraints. He would wait for it to calm down before delivering another blow, hitting it as hard as possible. He wasn't thinking of any particular person or thing, he was simply enjoying the act of punching: the tension in his muscles, the feeling of his fist making contact, and the resistance of the punching bag.

He had no idea how much time had passed since walking into the room. Ever since his birthday his mother had been letting him stay at the base later and later. She had tried to make him feel better, but quickly realized that nothing she said was going to help. The only thing that seemed to make him feel better was being alone.

The lack of windows in the training room meant that he had no idea what time it was, but it was probably dark outside. He should be heading home, but all he wanted to do was get lost in his actions – the slow deliberate punch that you never had time to do in an actual fight.

When he heard the door open he ignored it. It was probably Calypso, who he didn't want to deal with. Every few days she'd try to make him realize what a jerk he was being, and he was tired of it. Eston had been keeping his distance, just as she'd predicted, and she was angry that Nathan had let things get so bad. He didn't care anymore.

His whole life had been ruined and there wasn't anything he could do about it.

"Nice form," a voice behind him said.

Nathan froze in place. He recognized the voice, but it couldn't be… Carefully, as if moving too fast would alarm the person behind him, he turned around.

"It's good that you're practising so intently," Magnus Erikson the Second said, stepping further into the room. "The instructors say that you're a good fighter, but you should never rest on your laurels. There's always room for improvement."

"Th– Thank you, sir," Nathan replied, not sure what else to say. He couldn't believe that he was alone in a room with the most powerful man on the island.

"I hear that you've been having some trouble lately," Magnus said. "While there are many other duties for me to attend to, I felt as though I should personally see to this matter. After all, I'd hate for a promising young fighter to fall behind."

Nathan bowed his head low. "I'm sorry, sir. I'll do better."

"No," Magnus held up a hand for him to stop bowing. "I didn't come here to listen to you spout empty promises. We're going to talk this over until you've found a way to move past it. Now, what's the problem?"

It was so simple and stupid that Nathan suddenly felt too ashamed to put it into words.

"It's because you didn't get an element," Magnus said for him.

He gave a half-hearted nod.

"You know, my great-grandfather didn't have an element, and he managed to lead this island and free us from the tyranny of The Council. I don't have an element, just like him, but does that make me any less qualified to lead? No. People follow me because I have their best interest in mind, and because they know it's the right thing to do."

"But without an element I can't be as effective as the other soldiers. They'll always have an advantage because they've got a built-in weapon. If an Elemental loses their sword in a fight they can still defend and attack, but I don't have that."

Magnus considered his words. "You have a point. However, from what Kennedy tells me, you're an excellent hand-to-hand combatant, so never think of yourself as lacking a weapon. Nathan, I'm glad that you feel so strongly about helping the cause, but you can't let this obstacle defeat you. You need to figure out a way to turn this disadvantage into an advantage."

"But how am I supposed to do that?"

"Think of it objectively. While everyone else is splitting their concentration between element, weapon, and hand-to-hand training, you only have two disciplines to focus on."

For the first time since his birthday, Nathan saw a glimmer of hope for his future.

"Also, our scientists have proven that Elementals can't use their powers if they can't concentrate," Magnus continued. "So learn how to distract them, and find ways to turn their advantages against them. Show them that you're the better fighter and that you always will be, element or not."

A broad smile crossed Nathan's face. "Thank you, sir. It really means a lot that you came here to talk to me. I feel much better."

He reached out and placed a hand reassuringly on Nathan's shoulder. "Remember, heroes are defined not by how easy their lives were, but by the adversities they managed to overcome."

Ø

The talk with Magnus raised Nathan's spirits considerably. Instead of sulking, he became more focused. Eston was still avoiding him, but Calypso couldn't help remarking that he'd certainly changed his tune.

Although he suspected that his mother had a hand in it, Nathan didn't tell anyone about the talk or the fact that Magnus had sought him out directly. It was something he didn't want to share with anyone else, lest they ruin it. After the talk, he set about on his new mission – to be a better fighter than any Elemental. He studied their fighting styles, their strengths and weaknesses, and whenever someone tried to use their element against him in a fight, he made sure to take them down.

After four weeks, he was feeling more like his old self. His determination was back, and he was once more at the top of his class for weaponry and combat. One night he was in the weapons room, training late, when someone else came into the room. He was expecting his mother, so when he looked back he was surprised to see Magnus. As Magnus walked up to him, Nathan noticed that he was carrying a small box.

"I've been hearing good things," Magnus said as he drew closer. "Kennedy and your mother speak highly of your renewed commitment to training."

Nathan bowed his head respectfully. "It's all thanks to your talk, sir. I really needed to hear that."

He smiled. "It's part of my job to make sure that everyone on this island is achieving their full potential. We have big plans coming up and we'll need everyone at their best."

Nathan wanted to ask what the big plans were, but Magnus continued talking.

"Since you've been doing so well, I thought that you deserved a reward."

He held out the box. Nathan laid the practice sword on the floor and hesitantly took the gift. The box was made of dark wood; eight inches long, six inches wide, and four inches tall. He had no idea what could be inside.

Carefully he lifted up the lid.

"Ever seen a weapon like that before?" Magnus asked.

"Only in pictures." Nathan stared at the object in the box. It was entirely made of metal – smooth and sharp at the same time.

"The Council outlawed all projectile weapons after the Last World War, and while I can understand their reasoning, I feel that there are certain circumstances where a projectile weapon might be useful. Perhaps when one is fighting an Elemental who is able to set you on fire with a mere thought?"

A smile spread across Nathan's face.

"I'm having a practice version made up for you. It might take some time to get used to the weight and balance, but I have the utmost confidence in your abilities."

"Thank you so much, sir." Nathan took out the weapon and held it in his right hand. It was heavier than it looked, but easy to hold. He instantly felt more powerful.

Magnus smiled, pleased that his gift was so well received. "I'm certain you'll do great things in the future, Nathan. I've always been of the mind that if the world isn't fair, you have to learn how to take matters into your own hands. Never let someone else tell you what you can and can't achieve."

The smile grew wider as Nathan lifted the weapon, aiming it at an imaginary target in front of the wall. With this gun in his possession, he'd never feel weak or helpless again.

This wasn't the path he thought he'd be taking, but maybe it would end up being a better, stronger path.

The Devil's Mark

She had been watching the Eastern sky for the past hour, her eyes wide with fear and her fingers laced together tightly in silent prayer. At the first sight of grey smoke rising in the distance, she felt a sharp pain in her chest and her upper body crumpled, her shoulders drawing together as if to protect her breaking heart. Holding her breath, Amarylis watched as the smoke grew thicker and darker, until the blue sky was replaced by the ominous black cloud.

Tears welled up in her eyes. Turning away from the window, a trembling began within her, growing until it shook her entire body. Any minute now she expected to hear a pounding on the door, people screaming out for her blood, hands pulling her towards a pyre of her own, fire licking at her feet and smoke filling her lungs. Taking in a few deep breaths, she tried to calm herself down and steady her heartbeat. She told herself to concentrate on the silence around her. There was no mob, it was all in her mind. She was safe.

Only yesterday she'd been in the forest with Daisy, picking berries and flowers. They'd been laughing and sharing stories and gossiping about other people in the village. It had been a beautiful day, with the sun high in the sky and gentle breezes blowing through the trees. They'd emerged from the forest with full baskets and light hearts, but as they neared Daisy's home they spied a group of villagers gathered in front of the door. As they drew closer, the group turned on them, eyes narrowed and faces serious. Daisy whispered 'Oh, no' and then suddenly the group was upon her, pulling her away. Dropping her baskets, Amarylis started after them, but one of the men, Rowan, stayed behind and held her back. "She's been seduced by the devil," he told her. "I pray you have not fallen victim to his charms as well."

Hearing those words, Amarylis knew what she had to do. She had to turn her back on her friend otherwise suspicion would turn upon her and she'd end up under the judge's watchful eye. She stopped fighting and stood stock still. Once he realized that she wouldn't run away, Rowan let go of her. "I'm sorry you had to find out like this," he said before hurrying off after the crowd.

She stood there for a few more minutes, trying to calm her frantically pulse. Berries and flowers were strewn across the ground, but she made no move to pick them up. Instead, with a heavy heart, she turned her back on what had happened and headed home.

***

The trial was quick. Within an hour Daisy had been found guilty, sentenced to death, and the pyre had been built. It had been decades since the last witch had been burned, so the entire village planned on going. Amarylis had sat through the trial, under the watchful eye of her parents, but she'd refused to go to the burning and headed home as soon as the trial was over. As she stood in her parent's empty house, she wondered what she was going to do now.

Stepping away from the window, she went over the

words of the Elders in her head. *'On your twenty-first birth year you shall be tempted by the devil. He will entice you with great power, but do not say yes. If you succumb you shall be marked by him as one of his own and we shall know you by your mark. And thus shall you be burned for your weakness and your ashes scattered to the sea. And with your death the land shall be made pure once again.'*

It was the most important teaching within the village and one that everyone obeyed. Until Daisy.

Daisy's twenty-first birthday had been two months ago. At first, Daisy had said nothing, but one week after her birthday the two of them had been foraging in the woods when Daisy spilled her secret.

"It's not the devil," she'd whispered. "This power is from heaven itself. The Elders are lying because they don't understand what this power is, but I know." Then she'd put her hand out and suddenly a small patch of earth started to shake and move. Amarylis gasped, but Daisy smiled and told her it was okay. "Do you know how important this power is? I could help till the ground, plant seeds, and harvest food."

Amarylis could see her point, but she could also see the danger. "If anyone sees you do this..."

"I'll be careful."

"The Elders will never understand."

"The Elders need to stop living in the dark. So does everyone else in this village."

But the villagers weren't ready. Although Daisy tried to be subtle, suspicion soon grew about her sudden strange abilities with the crops. One of the older women took it upon herself to spy on Daisy, and one night she witnessed her using her power to till a field. The next day, the mob was formed.

During the trial Daisy had tried to convince everyone that her power was for good and that she had never done anything bad with it, but the Elders refused to listen. They showed everyone the mark on her arm, the one inch high brown square that hadn't been there two months ago. They said that she was trying to charm them, that she had been seduced by the devil and was trying to do the same to them, and their fear won out over her words every time.

Amarylis wanted to stand up and say that nothing about her friend had changed, that she was the same kind-hearted person she'd been before her birthday, and that this power was a gift and not a curse. But instead she sat silently and watched as her friend was sentenced to death.

And now, as the smoke began to slow and thin, she knew that the Elders had won. Daisy had lost her battle.

But the war wasn't over yet.

Amarylis had been born a month and a half after Daisy. Although she believed in Daisy's optimism about these powers, she knew better than to tempt fate. So when she received a vision of a great power and accepted it she made a promise with herself to never tell anyone else about it – not even Daisy. Turning her gaze to the candle sitting on the kitchen table, she narrowed her eyes and lit it with a thought, flame erupting from the wick. As Amarylis watched the candle burn brightly, her thoughts turned to the mark she had received upon gaining her power, the one inch red triangle on the top of her thigh, where no one but a spouse would notice. It wasn't the mark of the devil, it was a promise. It was a reminder that she needed to be very careful.

She thought about all of the lessons that the Elders

had taught them, how they tried to keep them on the path of what was good and right. But who were they to choose what that was? Was it good to burn well-meaning people alive? Was it right to live in ignorance and fear?

Although her power was not the same as Daisy's, it could be used for good. She could bring light and warmth, and help start fires for cooking. And yet it could do so much more than that. A smile broke out on her face as the flame burned brightly. Perhaps there was some merit to the Elder's teachings. *'And thus shall you be burned for your weakness, and your ashes scattered to the sea. And with your death the land shall be made pure once again.'* The Elders were the weakest people she knew, and by their own words weak people should be burned.

Amarylis smiled wider as she used her power to make the flame grow, consuming half the candle with one thought. It was time to make this island pure once again.

THE
SEGMENT DELTA ARCHIVES
READING ORDER

Ali House's epic dystopian science fiction series currently spread over the course of three short stories and two amazing novels, including her first: *The Six Elemental*.

Three of the shorts are available here in *The Lightbulb Forest*, and are also spread over multiple anthology collections such as *Sci-Fi from the Rock* and *Unexpected Stories*.

"Blending the worlds of science and mythology, *The Six Elemental* is a compelling page-turner with a heroine we can all relate to." -- Amanda Labonté, author of *Call of the Sea*.

"Kit Tyler is brought to life quite vividly and her journey through the fantastical, dystopian world filled with magical super-humans delves into subjects that run parallel to issues faced by young adults in our own world." -- Christopher Walsh, author of *The Gold & Steel Saga*.

What follows is the ideal reading order, as determined by the author.

"Twenty One"
695 years After Rebuilding
Zenyth Hansen has been eagerly awaiting her twenty-first birthday, when she'll finally receive an elemental power. Although she knows there's a small chance she won't receive anything, what she hasn't considered is the possibility that her twin brother might get a power and not her.

The Six Elemental
699 years After Rebuilding
Kit Tyler shatters conventions when she achieves the impossible and receives the power of all six Elements. She struggles to keep her newfound abilities secret as she tries to uncover what it means to be The Six Elemental.

"Acceptance"
688-698 years After Rebuilding
Nathan Roane wants to be the best, but when his twenty-first birthday goes past without receiving an element, he'll need to find a way to accept reality and prove his importance to the Tecken Army.

"The Devil's Mark"
703 years After Rebuilding
On an uncharted island in Segment Delta, Amarylis must cope with the harsh judgment -- and sentencing -- of her village's archaic laws.

The Fifth Queen
639 - 715 years After Rebuilding
Kendra Chen never considered her life to be particularly special, but when her uncle reveals a startling family secret, everything she thought she knew changes.

ENGEN TIMELINE

With over twenty novels spread over three different series by many different authors, the Engen Universe of titles is growing every day and into genres we couldn't have imagined! From the original ten book *Black Womb* thriller series, its crime novel sequel series *Xander Drew*, our flagship adventure title *Infinity*, or single-novels like *Jacobi Street* or *light\dark*, there's something in the Engen Universe for everyone with more books by more authors on the way soon!

...But how do the events relate to one another, chronologically? While some astute readers have guessed at the potential timeline (some accurately, some not), we're going to finally set the question of the Engen Timeline to rest.

Turn the page for an up-to-date guide of the ever-widening world of Engen, featuring the works of Ellen Curtis, Andrea Hackett, Ali House, Sarah Thompson, Jay Paulin, and Matthew LeDrew!

In the 10 Years Prior Black September

"Reptilia" by Matthew LeDrew
published in *light | dark*.
Danger descends on a small secluded town in the
form of a deadly virus with fantastic and terrible
side-effects. Can a small group of doctors escape
alive?

Compendium by Ellen Curtis
Three short stories forming the basis for the
Engen Universe's ties to suspense, genetic
engeneering, and the supernatural. Features the
stories "The Tourniquet Revival," "Falling into
Fire" and "At Midnight, the Dawn."

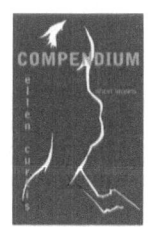

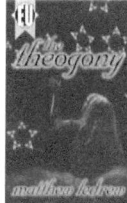

"The Theogony" by Matthew LeDrew
published in *light | dark*.
A tale of young Theo Flaherty of the *Infinity* series
and his time admitted against his will to the Black
Springs hospital, where he learns to paint, and
seeks out his father.

Black September

"Revving Engen" by Matthew LeDrew
published in *light | dark*.
A direct lead-in to both *Infinity* and *Black Womb*,
Tasha travels to Coral Beach, Maine on a hot tip
about a recently discovered young man with
incredible abilities.

Infinity by Ellen Curtis & Matthew LeDrew
Faced with a destiny he's uncertain of, the
enigmatic Victor must bring together four unique
people with very special abilities… or face the
tasks ahead alone. Guaranteed to excite!

Black Womb by Matthew LeDrew
Fifteen years ago, something happened in Coral Beach, Maine that resulted in the present death of a seventeen-year-old boy. Now four high-school students must try to solve the mystery… before the killer picks them off.

Jacobi Street by Matthew LeDrew
When a mysterious painting shows up at an art gallery he works at, Bob must work with Eddie and Sloan to track down its sinister origins and convince the people living on Jacobi Street of them, before its too late!

Transformations in Pain by Matthew LeDrew
When two girls are assaulted and one is hospitalized, the residents of Coral Beach must put their shared tragedies behind them and stop the man responsible, as well as unlock the secrets behind the true nature of the Womb…

Year One: October

Smoke and Mirrors by Matthew LeDrew
The approaching trial of Genblade brings closure to the people of Coral Beach, until people start showing up dead in the same manner they did when he was at large.

"Scarlett" by Andrea Hackett
published in *light | dark*.
Introducing Scarlett, the slightly damaged hunter on a mission to save others from the monsters from her past.

"The Inevitable" by Ali House
published in *The Lightbulb Forest*
A young woman must contend with the
emergence of a frightening new power alongside
the emotional high of a first date.

The Tourniquet Reprisal by Curtis & LeDrew
A man lives in Atlanta, Georgia that people
don't talk about, but everyone knows he's there.
He arrived a year ago and turned a gaggle
of uneducated youth into something new,
something to fear.

Roulette by Matthew LeDrew
As the teen suicide rate in Coral Beach starts to
climb astronomically fast, Xander travels to Los
Angeles to fight his most terrifying adversary
yet… and learns that the only thing worse than
looking for release… is finding it.

Year One: November

Exodus of Angels by Curtis & LeDrew
Victor's enigmatic past is illuminated when
Jaycee accompanies him to visit a new friend
in the paliative care ward of the Black Springs
hospital, where Theo also happens to be
searching for a cure for Leigh.

Ghosts of the Past by Matthew LeDrew
Coral Beach faces its most awesome threat when
one of Engen's past mistakes is unleashed upon
the unsuspecting populous. Friends and enemies
unite to fight a common enemy… but will even
that be enough?

Touch Your Nose by Matthew LeDrew
Simon Monk must infiltrate the San Fransico
branch of Shane Industries, a massive company
with deep ties to the Engen Universe. Where do
his true loyalties lie? And can he get out without
causing harm?

Ignorance is Bliss by Matthew LeDrew
After being set through the ringer one too many
times, Xander decides that his life with Julie
needs a little more attention... which is bad news
because a new villain has come to town with his
sights set on Adam Genblade.

"Gristle While You Work" by Jay Paulin
published in *light | dark*.
A short story centering around the rise of a new,
and possibly cannibalistic, serial killer in the
Engen Universe.

Becoming by Matthew LeDrew
For months Xander Drew has been doing his
level best to keep the streets of Coral Beach clean,
which means it's time for the forces of darkness to
strike back... all at once.

Inner Child by Matthew LeDrew
Julie is hospitalized with life-threatening wounds
to both body and soul. But the real threat comes
from the hospital walls themselves, as a demonic
presence makes itself known to Xander and his
friends.

End of Year One

Gang War by Matthew LeDrew
The Tees, a homicidal gang of evil men, has finally been taken down by Xander Drew. But his victory is short lived, as retired Tees are mysteriously killed. With a town of suspects, anyone can be the culprit… including one of their own.

Chains by Matthew LeDrew
Sociopath Derek Smith has been freed from prison and is praying on the weak; and none are weaker than August Styles: a pregnant girl with Down Syndrome who has run away from home.

"Omega" by Ellen Curtis
published in *light | dark*.
A sinister division of Engen begins a series of experiments on pregnant women in a fashion eerily similar to those that created the original Black Womb project.

The Long Road by Matthew LeDrew
Xander meets the American people — and realizes that the world is harsh and wicked, but can also be soft and gentle, even loving. Xander Drew comes of age on the road, and sets his new direction.

Year Two

Cinders by Matthew LeDrew
Detective Horton enters a violent and dangerous world he didn't know existed beneath the veneer of order and structure that he has based his entire deductive method around.

Sinister Intent by Matthew LeDrew
One of the killers Detective Horton could not catch has resurfaced: a serial killer who flaunts his sinister intent in front of the Los Angeles Police Department, making it so that no one is safe.

Faith by Matthew LeDrew
Xander's mysterious and troublesome past returns to haunt him on the streets of Los Angeles; a place where even more people can get caught in the crossfire of the games of death and deceit that makes up his life.

Flickers in the Night by Matthew LeDrew
Lisa Rowdan is hunted by her haunting -- and powerful -- ex-boyfriend Ryan through a lonely city street. Can she escape him?
One of over twenty great sprine-tingling short stories!

Family Values by Matthew LeDrew
Xander and his new friends Crowley, Lisa, and Tim investigate a series of kidnappings and murders that stretch back decades, all of which have the same similar twist: victims being found after years of being missing.

The Future

"Remers" by Sarah Thompson
published in *light | dark*.
In the not-too-distant future of the Engen Universe, young athletes are the targets of a scouting program to create the next stage of super soldier with cybernetic enhancements.

HEED THE CALL

After a heated fight at sea between twins Ben and Alex, Ben vanishes from their boat without a sound or even a ripple in the water. Unwavering in his dedication to find his brother, Alex begins the adventure of a lifetime armed only with the help of a local girl named Meg and his own mysterious musical abilities… the key to which, and to the mysteries that surround him, may be tied to the alluring song of the dangerous girl he finds among the ocean's frothing waves.

"A mysterious figure in the ocean, a suspicious loss in the waves, a riveting treasure hunt, and surprise after surprise, how could anyone not want to read this novel?"

~Alice Kuipers
author of Life on the Refrigerator Door

"Loved this book and can't wait for the next one."

~Helen Escott
bestselling author of Operation: Wormwood

"It's been a while since I've read an entire book in one day, but…Whenever I tried to put it down, it would call out to me, luring me back like a siren's song."

~Ali House
author of The Six Elemental & The Fifth Queen

ABOUT THE
AUTHOR

Alison House is an Award-Winning, Best-selling author, a playwright, a traveler, and a reader.

A native Newfoundlander, House is a graduate of the Fine Arts program at Sir Wilfred Grenfell College (MUN). She currently resides in Halifax, Nova Scotia, where she works in arts administration and spends more time than a person should in and around theaters.

House won the December 2018 Kit Sora Prize, which celebrates authors throughout Canada. Her short fiction has appeared in every issue of the *From the Rock* anthology series, as well as *Bluenose Paradox* and the *Kit Sora Artobiography*.

Her novels include *The Six Elemental* and *The Fifth Queen*.